MRS CALDER AND THE HYENA

Marjorie Ann Watts trained as a painter and illustrator with Edward Ardizzone and Harold Jones, then worked as an art editor and typographer. She left publishing to work as an illustrator (on books such as Catherine Storr's *Marianne Dreams*), before beginning to write and illustrate her own books for children. She has also written a novel and a guide to European painting for young people. Her father was a *Punch* cartoonist and graphic artist, her mother wrote her first book at eighty, and her grandmother founded PEN, as well as writing several volumes of poetry and twenty novels. She lives in London.

Mrs Calder and the Hyena

— stories —

MARJORIE ANN WATTS

for Simon

First published in Great Britain in 2025
by CB editions
146 Percy Road London W12 9QL
www.cbeditions.com

SC&JL

'Mrs Calder and the Hyena' and 'Birthdays' were previously published
in *Are they funny, are they dead?* (2010)

Printed and bound in the UK by CMP Books

ISBN 978-1-73942-6-7

Contents

Mrs Calder and the Hyena

'Is that true, mother? Or have you made it up?'

Elinor drummed her fingers on the table as if she could hardly bear to remain seated a moment longer and stared round the littered kitchen. Bottles, ash spilt along the window sill, and what was that brown substance in the appalling saucepan in the sink, the dish on the draining board? The room stank. She turned again to her mother.

'He's just a tramp, isn't he?'

'Tom? He's educated,' Mrs Calder said.

'Oh?'

'We have long conversations,' her mother said. 'In French. More coffee?'

She took out her cigarettes. How have I come to have a daughter like Elinor, she thought; although when she remembered darling Rupert's insistence all their married life that facts are facts, no monkeying about, perhaps Elinor was more explicable. Mrs Calder smiled. Rupert had had so many other qualities.

'A tramp,' Elinor said again, her face like a block of wood.

'Polish,' her mother replied mildly. 'A dispossessed child. After the camp, he started walking and he's never stopped. Not much younger than me and he knows nothing else. You couldn't expect him to live in a hostel now.'

'No one would have him,' Elinor said. 'Drunk, filthy. Where does he sleep?' Mrs Calder did not reply and Elinor added, 'Catholic, I suppose. Hasn't he got a family?'

'Well, I'm a Catholic –' Mrs Calder began.

'Oh Mother, you're not! How can you say that?'

'He sleeps in the churchyard. In the derelict bit at the top.'

Mrs Calder picked up their coffee cups. Why does she come, she thought, carrying the tray over to the draining board. She wondered if Elinor would notice if she took out the half glass of gin she had behind the parsley in the fridge? It's a mistake, letting her have a key to my flat, she thought, opening the fridge door, I'll have to get it back.

'That coffee has made me thirsty,' she said. 'Do stay, dear, but I have to leave you shortly.'

'Where are you going?'

'Well, my Californian admirer –'

'Mother! Don't you think it's, well, dangerous? Just going off for the afternoon with someone you have only met on the telephone? You hardly know him . . . I mean, who is he? Do you know anything about him?' Elinor sounded aggrieved.

'He's a Calder,' her mother said. 'Wants to trace any members of his family over here. He knew your father, slightly . . . through the university. He is an academic too.'

'Well, I hope you are not going on the Underground,' Elinor said, picking up her keys. 'Do you want a lift?'

'It's the opposite direction.' Mrs Calder glanced behind her and stood for a moment gazing towards the door, the hall beyond. 'Did I tell you I saw a hyena on the common yesterday? It growled at me.'

Elinor stared at her mother.

'A *hyena*?' She still was never sure what was serious, what was a joke. 'What on earth do you mean?'

'Always a little on the edge of my vision, but definitely getting closer.'

'What?'

'Of course we are near the zoo up here, and there's all this rubbish everywhere,' Mrs Calder murmured as if to herself. 'I heard it laughing – which makes a nice change.'

She looked directly at her daughter, her eyes gleaming behind her spectacles.

'Actually, hyenas *can* be dangerous,' she said after a pause, 'should one be unprepared.'

Driving home, Elinor considered the problem of her mother. She wasn't well; indeed, she looked obviously ill, had for some time – although she refused to discuss it. She's so irredeemably balmy, *potty*, Elinor thought; always had been. Brief but humiliating scenes from childhood crowded into her mind; her mother, the looks people gave each other; the over-active imagination, fabulation, eccentricity – how had she got away with it? Charm, thought Elinor bitterly, but there was a different dimension now. Bob said it was senility, but then he had never got on with his mother-in-law.

She is so, so . . . what was it? Unreliable, irresponsible – *mad*, thought Elinor, hooting at the red Audi in front, some idiot who didn't know right from left. Her mother drank, certainly more than was good for her, neglected herself. She wondered whether she had kept the last appointment at the hospital? What it would be like when she was gone, dead, finally extinguished?

For a moment, the neat suburban house waiting twenty miles out of the city, lovely lawns perfectly in place, shining windows, brick path up to the front door clean and swept – Bob liked things well done, was a fanatic about his garden – for a moment the whole image faded, became paper-thin, void.

'It's my home, I love it. It's what I want,' she said aloud to the passing traffic. Resentment flared comfortingly. She's mad; she'll say anything, *anything*! All these ghastly fabrications, you never knew where you stood. The Californian, for example. Which was worse? – that her mother had invented him or, at over seventy, had actually gone to bed with a total stranger in the middle of the afternoon at the Savoy Hotel, as she boasted to everyone? As for that awful game in the Underground – pathetic, obscene. She and Bob had discussed it at length with various social worker friends and decided that some old people got like this. Always harder for the carers anyway, muttered Elinor savagely, hooting again at the man in the Audi, right-hand indicator still flashing meaninglessly. At least Mother doesn't drive, she thought, overtaking him at last in a satisfying surge of speed as she reached the dual carriageway. What a relief to get going and think about something else; although she would have to get in touch with the hospital again. Bloody hyenas!

Mrs Calder retrieved the tumbler from behind the parsley, added more gin and seated herself on the stool by the kitchen window. Most of the flat was dark, inward facing, but from her kitchen and at the height she was she looked straight out into the western sky and, if she wanted, halfway across London. At night, low on the horizon over to the left, the yellow lights of Heathrow winked and glowed in interlocking chains of topaz. In the day, large aeroplanes made their way sedately across her line of vision, very often close enough to see the particular markings: the red leaf of Canada, white cross of Switzerland. Glass in hand, Mrs Calder would sit by the window imagining the passengers: the myriad hopes, fears, jealousies, impending tragedies, joys travelling slowly through the air towards their various consummations.

Recently she had begun to watch the sky itself more closely. About a month ago, she could have sworn to having caught sight of some indistinct figures sitting on a large cumulus cloud drifting ponderously but at speed in a south-westerly direction. One of them had looked very much like Rupert – although he isn't exactly a cloud man, as she had said to herself at the time. She had stopped watching the airliners in the hope of seeing this phenomenon again. Naturally she hadn't mentioned anything to Elinor.

Mrs Calder stood her glass in the sink. A pity Elinor hadn't any children; or perhaps it was a good thing? Preferable for the children, she thought, as she let herself out of the flat.

Down in the street it was very warm, a perfect June day. Like we used to have, Rupert and I, she thought as she walked between the lines of parked cars – a tall, imposing, rather untidy figure in tennis shoes and a creased floral dress, the hem of which was beginning to unravel. Other pedestrians hurried past her somewhat apprehensively, aware perhaps of the intense scrutiny that one and all were subject to.

'You are not locking those gates, are you?' She had reached the entrance to the parish churchyard, all shadows and dappled sunlight. 'My husband is buried in there . . .'

It was not the vicar, who she knew by sight, but some plump, moustachioed, too-well-dressed young man who turned abruptly at the sound of her voice. She waited, swinging her bag.

'Tramps!' he said, fiddling with a chain and padlock. 'Not to mention kids. And the litter!'

'I imagine Golgotha must have been knee-deep in litter,' Mrs Calder said. The young man eyed her, frowning.

'We are having problems.'

'I thought problems were His speciality? Although' – she inclined her head towards the newly painted gleaming church beyond the trees and railings – 'I am not convinced that He, or She, would feel much at home in there, are you?'

'We've had dogs in here too,' the young man said.

'What makes you think it's dogs?' She stood watching him struggle with the padlock, an odd speculative smile lighting up her face.

'How old are you?' she asked suddenly. He was not to know of course, but in her mind's eye she had removed the impeccable suit he wore and replaced it with a leopard-skin leotard: with his moustache, and dark hair parted in the middle, he made a good, if plump, Victorian high-wire acrobat. Oh, wait! She had forgotten the black polished shoes. She removed these too, then changed her mind; replaced the shoes, socks, took away the leotard and stood gazing at him, her grey spiky hair lit up and made almost gold by a shaft of light striking through the dense shadow of the cedars under which they stood.

'I'm not locking these gates,' the young man said with irritation. 'Just trying out the key. Your handbag is open, you know.'

Elinor was right about one thing, thought Mrs Calder,

walking away from the churchyard towards the Avenue. It was a game; but a good one – and quite a challenge to play. Anywhere would do, but the Underground was certainly one of the best places: people tended to stay put, you could see them, get a good view. Buses were more problematic.

A row of naked people sitting opposite one in the tube was entertaining; but that wasn't the object of the game, as she had sometimes tried to explain.

'But Mother! It's, well . . . *kinky*, it really is.' Elinor had sounded quite shocked.

'Well, they don't know,' Mrs Calder had said. 'Very discreet, really.'

'Surely there are more interesting things to – to think about?' responded Elinor primly. 'Why don't you read, if you must go on the Underground?'

It was a different doctor today. He sat at a desk, white coat on the back of his chair in the centre of a large bright room – windowless, Mrs Calder noticed – talking to a double semi-circle of students. She disliked him immediately.

'. . . a lady of seventy-six . . . the carcinoma is beginning to affect her grip on reality which, to say the least – ' He broke off, gesturing vaguely at a chair set at an angle in front of him as Mrs Calder walked in with the nurse.

'Good afternoon, Mrs Carter.'

'Calder. Good afternoon,' Mrs Calder said to the room in general, fishing for the packet of cigarettes in her bag.

'This is a non-smoking hospital,' the consultant said, not meeting her eye. Mrs Calder glanced at him again as she sat down – a tall, grey-haired man in a crisp blue-and-white shirt, immaculate tie, smiling at her without humour. Automatically she removed his shirt.

'We have had the results of your scan,' he said, picking up some papers. 'A bit inconclusive. We would like you to come in for a few tests. Do you live alone?'

Mrs Calder gazed at him. A hairy chest, she thought. How surprising. She hung a medallion on it. Pity she couldn't see the rest of him.

'I have my devotees,' she said. 'And then there is the hyena.'

'Your daughter is worried about you, Mrs Carter.'

'Calder. She thinks I am potty.' Holding an unlit cigarette between thumb and forefinger, she blew imaginary smoke out of her nose and watched as it drifted in two fine skeins towards the ceiling.

'Well, we would like you to come in here, next week. Just a few tests, so we know where we are. I'll explain . . .' Mrs Calder stopped listening. She found it strange that it should look as if there were sunlight in a room with no windows – as well as the sun, long grass, flowers. Rupert loved long grass in the summertime – and me, in the grass, she thought. Smiling, she changed the nurse's starched cap into a butterfly, frail white wings spread out and palpitating. Summer, green and lush, stretched across water meadows into the shade of willows. She could smell it.

'. . . and hope to be able to help you.' She heard the consultant's voice as if from another planet. 'Will you see Admissions on the way out? Nurse will take you down, help you with the forms.'

'Some people hear the hyena's howling as fiendish,' Mrs Calder said. 'I hear it as laughter.'

★

Outside the hospital the road, choked and grinding with traffic as usual, descended by degrees in an almost unbroken line towards the city. Waiting for the traffic lights to change, Mrs Calder saw with pleasure that the pavements on either side, broad and level at this point, were crowded and spilling over with an excess of humanity. The sun has brought them out, she thought, watching a group of old Chinese women, a black youth laughing by the flower stall. She crossed the road, joined the general movement down the hill, progressing slowly and deliberately like some gaunt flamboyant ostrich or crane picking its way along a public path at the zoo.

She must have been walking for over an hour when she felt the first spot of rain. The sun still shone with an intense yellow light on the tower blocks up-ended on the horizon, but behind them the sky was black; she saw a thread of lightning dart from one side to the other and thunder rumbled over her head somewhere. It began to rain heavily, the pavement rapidly becoming slippery, shining under her feet like a mirror. Coming at this point to an opening in the high brick façade of the street she saw, beyond a grimy patch of courtyard, a few geraniums in tubs, a notice which announced: 'Welcome to this Historic Church.' It was as good a shelter as any.

The building she found herself in was cool, dark after the hot street. Candles flickered in the draught from the door, their light catching sporadically on gilded crosses, haloes, wings, fragments on invisible walls. It was disturbingly quiet. The rubber soles of her shoes squeaked a little on the smooth tiles of the nave as she walked forward.

She remained for some minutes leaning against the altar

rail, her face raised towards the cross hanging above the darkened altar table. The small transparent red vessel containing the Host winked and shone exactly like the aeroplanes which swam past her window at night. As she gazed at it, she found it hard not to allow the thing to turn into a helicopter hovering above the altar, silently.

Her feet were hurting. She took off her shoes and sat down. The card placed beside the prayer book on the shelf in front of her read: 'Can we help? If you have problems we would be happy to discuss them with you.'

She sat listening to the soft hissing of the rain, pigeons up in the roof space. The silence, guttering candles, smell of incense and polish, the feeling of time suspended for ever, made her think of her convent, the happy face of the nun who had died at the end of the autumn term. She had forgotten her name.

'Hail Mary . . .' Mrs Calder remarked finally to the Child Queen of Heaven waiting on her dusty pedestal. 'You are very quiet. I am afraid there are no answers, my dear.' Absentmindedly she divested the little Virgin of her chipped blue mantle, fluted robe, expecting to find plaster beneath. 'Black lace!' she said, smiling. 'No one would have suspected.' Before she left, she lit a candle. Rupert would laugh, she thought.

The church clock was striking six as she reached the Avenue. Still very warm, the air smelt fragrant, fresh after the rain. She turned into the graveyard and, limping, pausing at intervals to rest, walked slowly along the grassy track which led to the part of the burial ground where Rupert lay.

Emerging from between outsize yew and holly, wet grass, she came suddenly upon some youths, their clothes streaked with paint, scrambling among the vaults and graves and kicking a tin or tins from one mossy level to another. As she approached they rushed away, laughing wildly and shouting to one another, leaping over the graves and bushes like a troupe of antelope. She saw at once that almost all the gravestones — the spaces were greater here — had been sprayed with paint: pale blue, orange, day-glo pink, the colours becoming more dazzling and outlandish the further she proceeded up the path. By the time she had reached the semi-derelict shelter or chapel where vases were stacked and Tom kept his bedding, she was walking through a punk-rocker's dream: zigzag red and black stripes, blobs of silver, blotches, star-bursts, the lot.

Cheerful, Mrs Calder thought, leaning for a moment against a cerulean angel with staring yellow eyes. Life, a bit of life! She laughed suddenly. Elinor's cross face had come into her mind. At the rear of the shelter, where grass clippings steamed in the sun and a blackbird rustled through last year's leaves and discarded wreaths, she found Tom, stretched out on a bench asleep or drunk or both. He lay like one abandoned by the tide, mouth open, greasy shirt unbuttoned and gaping, a sagging expanse of flesh exposed, stinking of alcohol and urine. Mrs Calder stood gazing at his mottled purple face, watching him.

'Tom?' She stooped swiftly, laid a hand on his stomach, whispered again, 'Tom?'

He stirred but did not wake, and after a moment she squeezed herself in at the end of the bench and sat clasping one of his ankles in both hands.

Like Tours cathedral, she thought, surveying the dazzling colours. She and Rupert had been to Tours on their honeymoon, and both loved bright colour; the stronger the better. Well, his grave was a masterpiece now.

Smiling and closing her eyes, Mrs Calder lifted her face up to the sun. Tom's wheezing breath, the ebb and flow of the traffic along the Avenue, murmur of bees in the privet hedge behind her, became as one sound. All the summers of childhood, of her youth, of her life with Rupert, seemed united in this one moment and eternally. Visions of an infinite blazing multicoloured graveyard stretching up into the sky and across the world swelled through her like a great chorus. In the centre of this immense fairground sat the hyena: a small figure at this distance, but she could hear it laughing quite clearly. I'll walk up there, she thought, when I have rested; in a moment I'll go up there. The thought filled her with an intense joy and excitement. Above everything she wanted to breathe that pristine celestial air, one with the quivering rainbows, prisms of colour radiating through and across the whole vast universe. Soon I will go, she thought again, her smiling face inclined towards the sky. The laughter became louder, nearer, increased a thousand-fold, filled her ears, her soul, her whole being, echoing through her and blotting out all other sound. She began to laugh too. Rupert! She cried suddenly, pulling herself upright. Holding out her arms and gazing enthralled at the path ascending before her, she started to walk forward.

Tom, who had retired to the chapel and his bedding roll in the small hours, left next morning by the side gate; so did not see Mrs Calder lying flat on her back in the long grass a few yards from the bench. And the vicar, rapidly inhaling on his cigarette as he took a short cut through the upper burial ground on his way to Matins, was so appalled by the unexpected riot of colour that he did not notice her either. So it was past eleven, the sun already climbing steeply, when one of the two policemen who had come to make a report on the vandalised graveyard observed two feet in sodden grey tennis shoes protruding from behind a particularly garish headstone.

Accustomed to death as they were, both men noticed how very peaceful the deceased appeared.

'Happy enough,' the older one remarked, bending over Mrs Calder. 'Smiling, like someone told her a good joke.'

Elinor, called in to identify her mother was struck by the smile at once.

'Looked as if she'd swallowed the cream,' she remarked angrily to Bob that evening. 'What on earth was she doing there? I suppose she couldn't have seen anything? That beautiful churchyard! And poor Dad's grave, it's going to cost the earth to –' She broke off. 'Bob, is there someone down in the garden? I thought I heard . . . heard laughter?'

They both listened, and Bob went to the window and opened it. Silence, nothing but the black warm summer night, curtains moving a little over the sill.

'I must have imagined it,' Elinor said, but uncertainly for her. It was quiet now, but she knew that actually she had heard someone laughing; quite a loud, disturbing, maniacal sound out there in the dark. And several times during the next few days she heard laughter again, faint but absolutely clear; she couldn't think why it upset her so much. Then, after a while, it ceased, and she forgot about it.

Blackbirds Singing in Granchester Square

I t was cooler in the shade of the big plane trees, and Anne felt herself unwind a little as she lay in the grass looking up into the freckled, shifting canopy above her. A blackbird was singing up there somewhere – or was it a thrush? A sweet, piercing sound carried on the warm air like a stream of iridescent bubbles.

She felt relatively secure, safe in the Gardens. Large wooden notices fixed to the gates proclaimed that these were 'Private Gardens for the Use of Residents Only – No ball games, dogs on a lead'. Because of the notices and the railings, the tall expensive houses facing each other round the square – and probably the gardener, who locked the gates at night and could be seen raking the grass or working among the dry sooty shrubs most days – Granchester Square Gardens had an exclusive, private feel. Occasionally, people used the footpath at the far end as a short cut to the High Street, but relatively few and mostly she knew them by sight: the old lady in black dragging her overweight pug behind her, the blind man she had walked past again today, a few nuns attached to the Oratory. Not many thought to leave the path and venture into the Gardens themselves. Even so, she took care to cover herself up with a scarf and outsized concealing sunglasses.

Reluctantly she sat up as her mobile chattered into life.

The producer and that script again . . . Why can't he leave me alone?

'Hello, Charlie.'

'Have you read it?'

'No.'

'Pete will be cross. What have you been doing all this time?'

'Nothing. Playing the piano.'

'The *piano*?'

'Yes. Why not?'

'Look, you are an actor, a professional −'

'I'm a musician,' she said.

He sighed.

'Annie, don't tell me you're "depressed" again?'

'Not depressed, bored.' She lay back in the grass, holding her mobile away from her ear. It's not the script and it's not Pete either, she thought − although he *is* impossible, but I can cope with him as long as I am not married to him. The truth is, it bores me. I just don't want to go on − in spite of everything. It's not my world . . . Never has been. She jammed the phone close again, and heard the end of Charlie's sentence:

'. . . just being neurotic. You'll be fine once you start.'

He always says that, she thought, switching him off.

The sun was still warm. At the far end of the Gardens she saw the blind man returning along the path carrying what looked like shopping. She watched his almost jaunty progress with a kind of wonder. He doesn't know what he looks like, who has seen him or is aware of his presence, she thought, feeling suddenly exposed on his behalf and wondering whether being recognised by everyone she met had become part of her DNA? What does it feel like to be so beautiful,

men and women sometimes asked? The question floored her
– whatever beauty she possessed was chance, nothing to do
with her. She certainly didn't *feel* beautiful – especially at the
moment. And despite the adrenalin rush of performance, and
the extraordinary effect her physical being had on so many
people, she had never become accustomed to being stared at,
her identity known wherever she went. If I was blind, she
thought, and could not know who was staring at me, gob-
bling up every tiny detail, gazing at this thing, this face, if it
all stopped, what would it feel like? What would *I* feel like?
Who am I anyway?

The Oratory bell was tolling quietly, the steady sono-
rous rhythm and distant murmur of traffic combined like a
soothing lullaby from a far-off valley. She closed her eyes
and began to count the slow deliberate strokes: one, two . . .
three, four . . . five, six . . . She was dozing off. Then, quite
close, someone coughed and she sat up quickly. A boy of about
ten was standing a few yards away holding on to a shiny new
bike several sizes too big for him, gazing at her with concen-
tration.

'Oh! I thought you were dead!' he said after a moment.
'Dad says you shouldn't sleep on the ground because of the
scorpions!'

She looked at him carefully. He was small, spindly, contemplating her calmly through hideous steel-rimmed spectacles
that magnified his eyes out of all proportion.

'Scorpions? In Britain?'

'We've just come back from from India. It's a fact,' he
said. 'Their stingers can kill you stone dead. No problem . . .
OK, I'll go now,' he added abruptly, hoisting himself up onto

his bike. He pushed down on the pedals and wobbled away across the grass in a sweeping unstable arc. People do die of course, she thought, watching him, and sometimes in public. She had passed a couple of paramedics dealing with a rough sleeper who had died a few doors away from her comfortable mansion block one cold night last winter. If her young inter-locutor had lived in India, perhaps he had become accustomed to seeing people lying dead on the ground?

A week later she saw him in the Gardens again, this time accompanied by a cross-looking girl. It was late afternoon, and they were rummaging their way towards her between the shrubs, apparently searching for something or someone. The boy reached her first.

'We are looking for our cat,' he said at once. 'He's gone missing!'

'They do go off sometimes,' she said. 'I am sure he'll come back. What does he look like?'

'Sort of black, he's run off because . . . because of the fire!'

'Fire?'

'In our house . . .'

'Your house? You mean your home –'

He nodded.

'There was a fire?'

'Everything burnt! *Totally!*'

'But – but that's terrible!'

'We had to escape out of the windows!' he said, gazing at her round-eyed.

By now the girl had worked her way round to the other side of the Gardens and was moving off towards the gates. She was shouting something.

'*Patrick*. Come *on!*'

'Got to go,' he said.

House totally burnt? Surely she should say or do something, but he was already running across the grass. Back at the Mansions, she asked the doorman if he knew of any recent fires in the neighbourhood. 'The near neighbourhood?' she added.

'Not to my knowledge, Miss,' he said.

'You can't hide away for ever, Annie,' Charlie said when he rang again a couple of days later. 'It's important you show your face –'

'It's not mine anymore.'

'You know its Pete's bash at the end of the week?'

'I'd forgotten.'

'Look, darling! Pete's made a great film, a box-office mega success, and you are wonderful in it, everybody is talking about you. Think of your career – *my* career, come to that! What? . . . What's divorce got to do with it? Get Harry to bring you –'

'Harry and I have split –'

'It's only a bloody party –'

'I told you – you've got to get me out of this film!'

'Don't be ridiculous! How can I? What will you do for money anyway?'

She cast around rapidly. 'I don't know. I have some savings. Play the piano? Teach?'

'That's absurd!'

'Why?'

'It's a wonderful part and you'd be raving mad not to do it,' he said, and rang off.

It's not absurd, she thought. I never wanted to be an actor – I am not an actor. It's an accident . . . and now I'm stuck. Gazing out of the window, words like money, admiration, praise, trundled through her mind, especially money. Seduced by mammon, she thought.

She went into the kitchen and got down the new coffee machine; measured out the coffee, then found there was no milk. I'll just walk round to the Indian shop, she thought. Instead, she spent nearly an hour at the piano, entranced by the mysterious harmonies of the piece she had set herself to learn. This is no good, she thought at last, I need some coffee. Get a grip.

She walked along the short stretch of pavement in the warm sunshine unrecognised and unmolested, called in at the little Indian shop for milk, only to find that they had run out. Not my day, she thought, turning into Artillery Place, the small close whose flagged central path served as a short cut into the High Street. The cottages here had come up in the world, with the result that now their gardens had become a sort of small but fecund urban jungle; the long narrow strips behind the picket fences on either side jumbled together and full of roses scenting the air, vegetables and salad leaves, rhubarb, tall tomato plants in pots. It's like a market garden, she thought. Why can't I live somewhere like this? My flat is like a prison.

Ahead, a large fig tree leaned out from its confined space, shading the narrow alley and obscuring her view. As she approached there was a sharp yelp and she heard the sudden crash of something metallic hitting stone. Walking a few paces further, she saw a bicycle lying in an awkward heap on the pavement under the fig tree, and caught underneath was the Granchester Gardens boy, legs and arms at odd angles.

The sister – if she was his sister – stood contemplating him, a mixture of irritation and concern on her face.

'He's learning,' she said.

'He seems to have learnt! Are you OK?' Anne asked.

'He's not allowed to ride his bike on a road,' the girl said.

'It's *not* a road,' the boy muttered, wriggling into a sitting posture and gazing around. Blood was beginning to trickle down from a gash on one side of his leg and the knee was badly grazed. He put a hand up to his face. 'I can't see anything.'

'Here!' Anne bent to pick up his glasses. 'These are OK . . . What's your name?'

'Patrick,' the girl said. 'Meet my stupid brother!'

'Look, blood!' He held up his knee dramatically.

'Where are you living, then?' Anne began tentatively. 'I mean, with the fire situation?'

'Fire?' the girl interrupted, frowning. 'What fire situation?'

'Patrick told me –'

'Oh, don't listen to *him!*' the girl said. 'I'm Lucy,' she added.

'Nice to meet you, Lucy,' Anne said.

They told her where they lived – one street away, just the other side of the High Street – and explained that the gardener objected to them riding on the grass in the square and had chased them off. So they had found their way into Artillery Close instead.

'I'll phone your mother, shall I?' Anne said. Silence.

'We could ring Dad?' The boy had scrambled upright and was holding a mobile in his hand.

'You can't,' the girl said.

'Why not?' Anne asked, looking from one to the other.

'There's Gran?' the girl said. 'We could –'

'No!' the boy shouted, and an argument began. In the end – and to prevent Lucy from stumping off – the easiest thing seemed to be to walk them and the bike the few hundred yards back to her flat, take them up in the lift, swab the knee clean with disinfectant and find some plasters.

'There, that looks better,' she said. 'Stand up and see what it feels like?'

'We'll go home now,' the girl said.

'Can I try your piano?' the boy asked suddenly.

Surprised, she opened it up for him and waited. He sat down, thought for a moment, and then began to play.

'Very good,' she said. 'Are you having lessons?'

'Sometimes . . . Is this your piano?'

'Yes.'

'It needs tuning,' he said. 'My dad could tune it for you if you like.'

'Is he a piano tuner?'

'Sort of.'

'We'll go home now,' the girl said again. 'Thanks for the plasters.'

'I'll just walk you to the High Street, shall I?'

'Actually he is an astronaut,' the boy said. 'He –'

'Oh shut *up*, Patrick!' Lucy said sharply, yanking at her brother's sleeve.

Together they went down in the lift, and she walked with them back through Artillery Row. Astronauts must have children, she supposed, glancing at Patrick. He had played through the Bach prelude as if he did it all the time.

They turned off just before reaching the High Street, and in a couple of minutes were outside the gate of a large shabby brick villa where there was no evidence of recent fire, although it could have done with a lick of paint.

'Where was this fire, then?' she asked as they walked up the steps.

'At the back,' Patrick said.

There was something familiar about the youngish pleasant face of the man who opened the door, but she couldn't place him. Patrick started gabbling about his knee.

'Dad! I fell –'

'Hold on, hold on. What happened?'

'He was riding on the pavement again,' Lucy said coldly. 'And this lady –'

'He's gashed his knee I'm afraid,' Anne said. 'But I've washed it, covered it up with a plaster –'

'I think it's broken!' Patrick interrupted. 'And the blood, Dad! *Gallons* of –'

'Well, you seem to be walking on it somehow? Thank you so much.' He was smiling at her. 'I hope he hasn't been a nuisance?'

'Not at all,' she said. 'I've enjoyed meeting them.' Where *had* she seen him before?

Walking back to the Mansions she considered the dreaming, speculative expression on Patrick's face as he had told her about the fire . . . and about India and the scorpions, the astronaut father. That man an astronaut? It seemed unlikely, somehow.

A couple of days later, she took the script out of the folder and read a few pages.

Perhaps I am bored *and* depressed she thought, glancing towards the window where sunlight streamed in, lighting up the dust balls on the carpet. I certainly don't laugh much these days (what is there to laugh *about*?). She had lost count of the occasions she had started reading Pete's script. Every time she tried, she had surfaced a few pages later thinking about an entirely unrelated topic. This morning was no different. Defeated, she took an apple and a couple of tangerines from the fruit bowl, tucked the folder under her arm and was already outside the flat and making for the lift when her mobile rang. Charlie – again!

'No!' she shouted into the phone. 'I haven't bloody read it! And yes, I am coming to Pete's thing!'

It was very quiet and at first glance the gardens seemed deserted. Then, as she walked towards the long grass under the plane trees, she saw the blind man, white stick beside him, sitting on one of the wooden benches a few paces further on. He must have heard her coming, because as she approached he called out:

'Excuse me, could I ask you for the time please?'

'A little after twelve . . .'

'Thanks.'

On the rare occasions when she saw anybody sitting on one of the seats, she always walked straight past whether they spoke to her or not, invisible behind her dark shades and swathed silk scarf. Now she stopped, contemplating the figure sitting in the sunshine: the ruddy, unlined, open face, untidy fair hair, fixed unseeing gaze. It can't be him, she thought . . . Patrick's father? She stood looking at him.

'Is it OK if I join you for a moment?'

'Please do.' He pulled his briefcase closer to him. 'I'm listening to the blackbird.'

'Blackbirds singing in Granchester Square!' she said. 'Sounds like a song . . . Actually, I think we have met before.'

'I thought I recognised your voice – '

'I brought your son back the other day. He fell off his bicycle.'

'Oh yes! That was you? Thanks again . . . Rather a melodrama, I'm afraid!' He smiled. 'But that's Patrick!'

'Is he alright?'

'Absolutely fine. He has been talking about nothing else – and your piano.'

'He told me it needed tuning – which is true! He seems very musical?'

'When one can get him to concentrate. I'm afraid he's rather all over the place at the moment.'

'I think I've seen you before in the Gardens sometimes?'

'Probably walking through on my way to work. I tutor the senior boys in mathematics at the Oratory.'

'Patrick has quite a lively imagination, doesn't he?' she said after a moment, remembering the astronaut story and the 'totally burnt' house.

'That's an understatement!'

They sat in silence for a while and she was on the point of asking about the fire when he said: 'Did you know that blackbirds are musical? It's thought they add a phrase to their song every season. One should be able to tell how old each individual is by how many musical phrases they have collected.' He smiled, looked in her direction with large blue apparently focused eyes. But he can't see me, she thought, so he doesn't know who I am. She was surprised at how relieved she felt.

'Well, I should be going. It's half term and there was some

idea that my kids would join me here today in the lunch hour, but I expect they've found something else to do.' He asked her whether she had children. When she said no, he smiled and said kids were wonderful but probably she had saved herself a lot of trouble.

'If you like singing . . .' He stood up and felt among the various papers in his briefcase before handing her a slip of paper. 'This is coming along next week: "Music at the Oratory". Patrick sings in the choir there and this time he has a solo part – if they haven't thrown him out by then!'

'That sounds dramatic?' she said.

He laughed. 'The more drama the better as far as Patrick is concerned!'

They said goodbye and she watched him move off towards the gate, white stick tapping the path before him. How long had he been blind? Had he ever seen his children's faces? He must have a wife, a partner?

On the way home she called in at the Indian shop to leave an ad for a piano tuner, and asked if the blind man was one of their customers.

'Robin, you mean?' Mrs Patel said immediately. 'Oh yes. Very nice. Got a lot on his plate, poor man.'

'What, for instance?' she asked. But someone else had come into the shop, and Mrs Patel's attention had shifted.

It was the evening of Pete's party. Six-thirty in his huge Pimlico mansion for drinks and then on somewhere later, food, a club – more drinking, if she knew Pete. I won't stay for all that, she thought.

She decided to call in at Luigi's and have a few nibbles and a glass of something herself to bolster her courage; then take a taxi, arrive late and leave early. Just put in an appearance to keep Charlie quiet, she thought.

Luigi's was crowded, although it was still so early. She often came here, met friends after the theatre, but mostly it was Harry, of course, or had been. A discreet out-of-the-way place, and so near the dark little basement flat which was his London pied-à-terre. Their usual – their *ex*-usual meeting place. Well, that was the past, thank God.

'Why are we doing this still?' he had asked last time. 'You and Pete – how long have you been divorced?'

'Two years.'

'Why can't I come to you, then? It's different for me, with –'

'Your wife.' She finished the sentence for him.

'Annie, what's the matter?'

She had pulled away from him then, pale and naked as she was, and walked over to the mellow-toned, scratched old up-right in the corner left behind by the previous tenant.

'This piano is the only good thing about your flat,' she said after some minutes. 'I don't know why you go on renting the place.'

Harry, half submerged among the cushions of the divan, lay watching her, arms behind his head.

'You'll have the neighbours in if you play like that.'

'This is how it is written,' she said. She hadn't seen him since.

Luigi appeared beside her table, pencil poised.

'Just a glass of something . . . A small glass,' she said. 'I have to go on – to –' She broke off as he turned for a moment to welcome new customers.

Generally Luigi put her and Harry in an alcove on their own, but that had gone tonight – anyway, Harry wasn't with her. She drank her wine slowly. If one was blind she thought, what about food? You would put stuff into your mouth without knowing what it was? Drop something and not see? Arrive somewhere stained with blackberry juice or gravy?

Looking from the window of the taxi a few minutes later, she saw the Thames glittering beyond the Embankment. The traffic had cleared and an erratic moon, full, waxen, dodged to the far side of Big Ben and back again as they swung round Parliament Square and on towards the Pimlico mansion where they were to celebrate last year's box-office miracle movie.

'Don't I know your face?' the taxi driver asked.

'The face that launched a thousand ships! . . . Keep the change!' She gave him the famous smile, crammed on her glasses and ran up the steps, leaving him gazing after her.

The big downstairs rooms were already jammed with people, noise like a solid wall. Anne drew herself up, took a deep breath and walked in through the door, the crowd turning to gaze at her as if some miraculous vision had appeared.

The first person she saw was Charlie, standing talking to a man in a red waistcoat.

'Darling, hi! Let me get you a drink? Good to see you. glad you made it.' Hands on her shoulders, he kissed her on both cheeks. 'Where's Harry?' and when she didn't answer, added, 'You look stunning, Annie. How are you?'

'Fine.'

The red waistcoat held up his glass.

'Ah! Annie Donohughe! I didn't quite recognise you . . . The shades? Many congratulations! What's next for you, then?'

Anne did not reply. Through a gap in the press of bodies, she could see Pete – some little trollop on his arm, laughing and gesturing dramatically as he told some outrageous story. Laughter sounded across the room and people smiled at each other, craning their heads to see what that joker Pete Donohughe was up to now!

'You were saying?' the red waistcoat prompted.

'Oh yes, the movie. Well, it's coming along . . .' She hesitated. 'Please excuse me, there's someone over there I need to say hello to. So nice to meet you . . . See you later, Charlie, maybe.'

The two men gazed after her as she moved through the crowd, pausing now and then to greet the people she knew.

'What's up with her, for God's sake?' the red waistcoat muttered, gazing after her.

'Wonderful actor but nobody gets near Annie Donohughe. Freeze you solid at fifty yards!' Charlie laughed. 'They're divorced now, of course. I don't know whether she minds or not. God knows I am having a hard enough job keeping her focused. She keeps telling me she wants to give up and be a bloody pianist, if you can believe it!'

Slowly Anne made her way through the crowded rooms, smiling and pausing briefly when people spoke to her. In the conservatory at the back of the house she found Pete's producer talking to a small group of technicians.

'Harry was here a moment ago,' he said. 'I think he was looking for you.'

The conservatory was a mass of trailing greenery, and a woman who had worked on the film as a designer called to her from behind one of the exotic ferns. It was as good a place as any to avoid Harry, and she sat for a while listening to some interminable nightmarish story about a handicapped child and a cheating husband until she could bear it no longer.

There was no one in the hall to notice her departure and, relieved, she closed the front door and stood in the portico breathing in the cool river air with its tang of salt and mud. Although it was still early, the street lights had come on, their reflections beginning to shine on the surface of the water.

'Annie! Hi!' Pete detached himself from a small group standing on the pavement. 'Where are you going?'

'Home,' she said.

'Oh, come on! You've hardly arrived. Anyway I want to talk to you.' Unrepentant, flushed with alcohol and larger than life, a big handsome confident man, her ex-husband blocked her path with easy good humour, smiling up at her. 'Most beautiful woman I ever married,' he said over his shoulder to the group on the pavement. It doesn't work any more, she thought. None of it works any more.

'Do you really have to go?'

'Yes.'

'I'll walk with you, find you a cab?' He laughed, face genial, mischievous. He never takes no for an answer, she thought.

'I am quite alright, thanks.'

'I can see that. Have you read the script yet?'

'No.'

'Why not?'

'I've been busy.'

Gripping her arm, he kept pace with her as she began to walk along the pavement, talking loud and fast like he always did. 'That part is made for you. Annie, don't be like this!' He halted abruptly, pulling her round to face him, fingers digging into the flesh of her arm. 'Mm, what's the perfume? God, you are the most sexy, maddening woman, why do you always give me such a hard time?'

'Let go of my arm, Pete – *now*!'

She crossed the road, took off her shoes and walked towards the Embankment, up Whitehall and into the crowds in Trafalgar Square, barefoot. With her shawl over her head and shoulders and her face obscured by glasses, no one recognised her; and she stood for a time watching a juggler perform in front of small crowd. The shining coloured balls pitched up one after the other very fast and seemed to hang in the air independent of any human agency. Over near one of the lions, a man selling frankfurters had set up a stall; she bought one, with some burnt onions, wrapped in a soft cotton-wool roll, and ate it as she sat watching the fountains, the wavering plumes glittering like diamonds. Come on, I can't loiter about here all night, she thought at last, and began to look around for a taxi.

She slept late, and next morning had just come out of the shower when the hall porter called her on the intercom.

'A young gentleman down here for you, Miss. Says he's your nephew. Patrick, is it?'

'Oh. Yes . . . Tell him to come up.'

'That fire,' she said when Patrick walked into the room.

'Our piano is burnt to ashes', he said, gazing at her sadly through the distorting lenses. 'Can I come and live with you?'

'*Me?*'

'I could play your piano.'

'You can play my piano any time . . . Why do you want to live here?' He didn't reply. 'What about your parents, your father? – Your mother? She wouldn't want you to live away from home would she?'

He stared at the floor. 'Our cat still hasn't come back.'

'But not because of a fire.'

'My mother is dead,' he said.

Annie studied the thin pale face. Was he making this up too? It's getting out of hand, she thought.

'Patrick, I'm going to phone your father. What's the telephone number?'

He gazed round the room vaguely. 'Can't remember,' he said. 'I'll go back and get it shall I?'

'We'll go together' she said.

'Hello Gran,' Patrick said when the front door opened. An elderly grey-haired woman with eyes too close together in a long aggrieved face stood there frowning at them.

'Why aren't you at school, Patrick?' she said at once.

'Staff study day,' he said without hesitation, and walked past her into the hall. She won't buy that, Anne thought.

'The school *telephoned*, Patrick. Twice!' The grey haired woman called after him. 'You have missed a rehearsal!' But there was no reply and she turned back to Anne. 'Have you come about the advertisement?'

'No, not really. I'm just a friend –'

'My son-in-law is advertising for another help but they are all foreigners, of course. Nobody wants to work these days.' A door banged shut upstairs. 'That boy is out of control,' she continued. 'Just comes and goes as he sees fit. It's not right!'

She began to close the front door.

Poor Patrick, she thought, walking home. But I suppose she was worried? Back at the flat she took out the flyer Patrick's father had given her and looked at it more carefully; saw that as well as various choral works, PATRICK TUCKER would be singing solo in the Oratory concert on Saturday evening at seven o'clock – the day after tomorrow, in fact. Perhaps I'll go, she thought.

She heard the Oratory clock striking one o'clock and was preparing to heat up some soup when the phone rang.

'Oh, Robin Tucker here . . . Patrick's father. Do forgive me for telephoning you – I don't even know your name – '

'Anne . . . Donohughe,' she said. 'It's OK.'

'I was in the Indian shop and Mrs Patel had your number. I just wondered if Patrick might be with you? He skipped this morning's rehearsal, and now he has disappeared.'

'Yes, he was here earlier – I brought him home. He's not here now . . . Do you want me to go and look in the Gardens? See if he's taken his bike there?'

'Well – '

'I don't mind at all. Better give me your phone number so I can ring you back?'

Immediately he had rung off, she got out her keys and set off for the Gardens; walked all round calling his name, but of course Patrick was not there. Probably had a row with that dreary grandmother, she thought; he'll come back. She rang the number that Robin Tucker had given her and left a message. Then spent the rest of the afternoon at the piano; and when, at six o'clock, Robin Tucker rang again, she had almost forgotten about the existence of Patrick.

'I thought you would like to know that the wanderer has returned,' he said.

'That's a relief. Has he told you what he has been doing?'

'Went to both ends of the Piccadilly line to see what they looked like . . . They are very cross at the school of course.' He hesitated for a moment. 'I – I, well, I am not sure if you know this, but the children lost their mother a year ago? And Patrick –'

'Oh, I'm so sorry! I thought he was making that up as well,' she said after a moment. There was a lengthy pause.

'Christina, our help, has had to leave recently, and well, I think it's unsettled him.'

'I am so sorry Is there someone else perhaps?'

'I am advertising for a mother's help, and my mother-in-law has been coming in from time to time. But, well –'

'Yes, I think I met her. What about the concert?'

'The day after tomorrow.'

'I'm looking forward to it.'

'I'll tell Patrick that,' he said.

I suppose I should offer to help, she thought after he had rung off, and laughed as she imagined Charlie's face if she told him that she had applied for a job as a mother's help.

Anne had never been inside the Oratory, and was surprised by the size of the place, its echoing gloomy splendour. The audience coughed and creaked on their hard chairs, waiting for the concert to begin, and she looked around for Robin but didn't see him anywhere. At last the lights dimmed and the choir master emerged from the shadows at the rear of the building, leading his choristers in their red robes and frilled white surplices in slow procession up the aisle to where the orchestra waited. Banks of candles cast a soft flickering light on the gold and alabaster of the high altar and on the upturned faces of the choir, and she saw at once that Patrick was standing in the centre of the first line of singers, his outsize spectacles glinting in the candle light. At least he made it to the performance, she thought, whatever had happened about the rehearsals.

A hush fell. Glancing at the programme, she saw that a Bach cantata was to come first, followed by one or two other items and then a sixteenth-century choral work. Solo soprano part, Patrick Tucker.

When Anne first heard Patrick sing, she thought her heart would stop. Those first piercing notes vaulting up effortlessly to the top of an impossibly high register made the crystalline purity of his voice seem barely human. She stared at the diminutive spot-lit figure, head back, glasses perched on the end of his sharp little nose, music held straight out in front of him. How was it possible that such a scrap of a boy could produce such a breathtakingly beautiful sound? Astonished and moved, she listened spellbound as the long sustained notes soared up, part of some other remote invisible world that one could only guess at. Truth laid bare, she thought.

It was a lengthy piece with many repeats, and each time it seemed impossible that any human voice, let alone a child as young as Patrick, could reach up to such a height. Yet, bell-like and clear against the colour and depth of the choral tapestry moving beneath, each time his unerring treble lifted up to the chapel rafters as if it was the easiest thing in the world.

When the lights came up at the end, she looked round for

Robin among the audience again, but did not see him; and it was not until she was leaving that she caught sight of Lucy and then him, standing by the wall just inside the entrance as the audience crowded past them towards the doors.

'Robin? That was wonderful!'

He smiled in her direction. 'I am so glad you could come!'

'He was amazing! You must be proud!'

'We had to handcuff him to my daughter Lucy to get him here for the dress rehearsal this afternoon!' He smiled wryly. 'The drama of live performance is one thing, hard work another matter!'

'Did you hear me?' Patrick asked the moment he appeared out of the crowd. 'I'm the only one in the choir that can sing that high C!'

'It was wonderful, Patrick,' she said again.

Beaming at her though his terrible glasses, he gave a little jump of excitement and joy.

'Was I good, Dad?'

'You were great, Patrick.' Robin rested his hand on the boy's head. 'I'm very proud of you. We all are!'

They walked together down the wide steps to join the rest of the crowd streaming out through the iron gates of the Oratory and on towards the High Street; stood together on the pavement for a while, talking.

'By the way, I meant to tell you,' Robin said, 'I'm a member of the Association of Blind Piano Tuners, so I could tune your piano some time if you want? Save you some money.'

She laughed at that, and the children, chattering and joking together, took their father's hands as they moved along the pavement. She watched them turn the corner into their road and had already started walking back, when Patrick came running after her.

'I forgot!'

'What?'

'Our cat's come back!'

'That's wonderful, Patrick! I told you he'd turn up.'

'Would you like to see him?'

'I would. Very much.'

'When?'

'Soon.'

'Tomorrow?'

She laughed. 'Very soon.'

In the morning, Patrick's face still vivid in her mind, she sat by the open window with her coffee, eyes drawn to the green tops of the plane trees just showing above the roofs of Granchester Square – where now the blackbird is singing, she thought, leaning back in her chair. Everything seemed suddenly remarkably simple and obvious to her as she remembered the high haunting treble soaring out over the darkened chapel. I can help them, she thought. Go round? Be there sometimes? Tomorrow, or the day after . . . Why not? And the children could visit? – Patrick and I can play four hands. Robin will tune my piano . . . We can take a picnic to the Gardens . . . She floated off into haphazard hazy speculation, everything possible, even likely, until some traffic noise in the street jolted her back into the room.

Focusing reluctantly, she saw Pete's script on the table under the window and picked it up. She stood holding the folder, gazing down at the street below and hesitating as the minutes passed. I'll read it tomorrow, she thought finally, slipping it into the drawer.

Untidy sheets of music lay in piles on the floor near the piano. She looked through them, slowly searching for the piece she wanted. At length, calmly and without haste, filled by what seemed to be some sort of unfamiliar but intense optimism or hope, she lifted her hands and began to play.

Thirty Years

If Jenny had known that she would run into Miriam in this posh north London coffee shop, she would have kept away.

'What are *you* doing here?' Miriam asked almost indignantly. 'I thought you lived in the country now?'

'We do,' Jenny said. 'But I'm visiting Lucy to give her a hand. Another baby at the end of the month. How are things? I haven't seen you for – it must be getting on for eighteen months?'

'More like two years . . . Not since you moved. Are you having something to eat?'

'No thanks.' Jenny glanced at her watch. 'I mustn't stay long.'

'Neither must I.' Miriam frowned, sipping her coffee. 'How's John?'

'Fine. Working too hard . . . I hardly see him.'

'I was very shocked to hear about Iain McAlpine's death'.

'Yes . . . Awful.' Jenny felt something in her spring to attention. Miriam and Iain's wife Helen had known each other in some previous life, and kept in touch intermittently.

'Did you go to the memorial? I was still out of the country.'

'Full of grieving women,' Jenny said lightly, and laughed.

'A man like that, bound to have – well, outside interests,

wide-ranging friendships. I mean . . . He was easily bored, had so many sides . . .' Miriam stirred her coffee and gazed at Jenny out of bland blue eyes.' Does she know something? Jenny thought suddenly. 'Not the best husband material,' continued Miriam, 'but I think they were happier in the last years. Closer. Of course it was difficult for her . . . You know. But Helen is strong. Actually, I was always rather fond of Iain.'

'Everyone was,' Jenny said. 'How are the children? What are they all doing?' But Miriam refused to be diverted.

'When did you last see Iain? I was in India when it happened. Such a shock – just to find out . . . casually, when I got back.'

'It must have been.'

'When did you – '

'Just a minute, Miriam, I need some sugar.' She rose from her chair abruptly. The images that had crashed into her mind, blotting out everything else, were so precise and vivid that she thought that everyone in the café must be able to see them, Miriam included: the club room, Iain's puzzled face, blurred incoherent speech as he fell sideways against her on the shiny leather settee; the man coming over from another table . . . 'I am a doctor, I think your friend is ill. Shall I call an ambulance?'

In Accident and Emergency, they had undressed him, laid him stretched out on the high bed, covered him with a red blanket.

'And you are?' The doctor who was examining him had stood back for a moment, looking at her. After a pause she said: 'We were lunching together, at his club. I'm a friend. He became ill and . . .'

There was silence in the room until the consultant said quietly, 'It's a question of who to inform.'

'Oh yes. His wife, I suppose?'

'Do you have the number?'

'Not on me.' Why did she say this? Of course she had the number. 'The club will know,' she said. Then she had handed his spectacles to a nurse, kissed him briefly on the forehead and left; walked down the long hospital corridor to the lifts, her shoes squeaking on the polished floor. Outside in the dark unfamiliar streets it was snowing.

'It was snowing!' she said loudly, suddenly aware of Miriam shaking her arm, talking to her.

'Jenny? *Jenny!* There's sugar on the table already. Are you alright, dear? What's the matter?'

'Nothing, I'm fine . . . Fine. I get these . . . this dizziness sometimes, and it is very hot in here. What were we talking about? How are the children? Did I tell you I am about to become a grandmother again?' Her voice trailed away until there was silence. Then she heard herself saying, 'Miriam, we are having a sort of party at the end of the month, it would be lovely if you could come?' (What was wrong with her? Why had she said this?)

That had been two weeks ago, and since then she had been unable to concentrate, keep her mind on anything sensible, practical, for two minutes at a time. My lost secret life, she thought; locked away for so long, and now the lid has blown off and I can't close it. Images kept crowding in and she would forget what she was doing; stand in the middle of the room with a tray, or some ironing, an ingredient for supper, remembering conversations or an incident of ten, fifteen,

even twenty years ago, in the minutest detail. Walking over
the rough grass of Hyde Park together – 'Your feet alright?'
Hands clasped tightly. Warm strong square hands, practical,
surprising. Sitting in deckchairs in the shade talking, catching
up on each other's lives; always laughing, happy, so happy.
Until she met Iain she had been on the shy, serious side, and
the humour, fits of delighted hilarity and laughter, silly jokes,
were new to her, a kind of revelation. Smiling at the memory
of it even now, it was as if she had been sleepwalking through
her life until then. And the excitement and danger of it! The
plans, plots, the scheming to be together against all the odds;
unfamiliar out-of-the-way places where nobody would know
her; getting to the rendezvous they had arranged – would he
be there? She remembered snow flicking against the wind-
screen, driving in the dark through white glittering woods
scribbled with black towards an unknown bridge, trying to
remember directions; and then, catching sight of him, pac-
ing up and down on the pavement of the bridge like a sentry,
breath rising in plumes on the frosty air.

'There was snow, deep snow! I didn't think I would get
through!'

'But you have! And we are here!'

Laughing like teenagers as they ran up the steps of the hotel,
serious adult faces assumed as they were shown to their room,
clutching each other shivering between the cold sheets; but
then, warming and quickening, her body opening to him like
a flower as he took her in his arms, the rest of her life spinning
away, blotted out by the whirlwind that overwhelmed them
both.

She had been back to the hospital, of course, walking into

the ward out of visiting hours like a thief in the night, afraid of meeting Helen. Whispered to him, held the awful cup with a spout, but he hadn't known her; had stared vaguely through her and then at the ceiling, mumbling unintelligibly. The next time he was unconscious, and she had fled to the shining empty hospital chapel, knelt sobbing and praying wildly, banging her head on the pew rail. When she returned to the ward, there was a curtain round the bed.

'Very poorly today,' the nurse said when she went to the desk. 'What was the name?'

'Just a friend,' she muttered and left quickly, hailing a taxi to take her to the station.

'You alright, luv?' the driver said, gazing at her.

'I've been visiting someone . . . Very ill.' Her throat was so constricted she could hardly speak.

'While there's life there's hope,' the taxi driver said. 'You see! You'd be surprised how often I drive people away from this hospital who tell me they'd given up hope, and all of a sudden there's an improvement . . . and then their loved one gets better! Honest! I see it all the time, all the time.' Absurdly – as she thought now – she was comforted. Two weeks later, travelling to a northern city where her husband was to receive an honour of some kind from the university there, he had looked up from his newspaper and said:

'There's a piece here about Iain McAlpine. Had a stroke and died, poor fellow. Did you know? We'll have to get in touch with Helen.'

Today her eldest daughter had driven out to see her, and they had spent lunch talking about Simon, the youngest of Jenny's children, trying and failing to become an actor.

'Poor Dad,' Viola said. 'Acting is not his thing at all. Nor mine, come to that. How is Dad, by the way?'

'Fine, I think,' Jenny said. 'Staying overnight again today, he is so busy. New York next week.'

'Well, lawyers at that level are always busy,' Viola said.

Lunch finished, they had moved to the garden, taken their coffee into the shade beneath the old pear tree which grew close to the house on that side.

'I went to see Lucy's new baby last weekend.' Viola's voice was cool. 'Screaming and hideous!'

'They do improve.'

'But five children?'

'Some women just adore having babies,' Jenny said, thinking that divorced Viola, with her high-powered job and regulation couple of boys packed off to school as soon as possible, certainly did not come into that category.

'Like rabbits,' Viola said. 'I hope she can afford it.'

'I shouldn't think so.' Jenny sighed, and they relapsed into silence. 'All that seems so long ago,' she said at last.

'Well, it *is* a long time,' Viola said. 'Forty years of marriage? My *God,* Mum!'

There was another lull in the conversation and Jenny thought, what would she say if I told her that for twenty-three years of it I had a lover who I adored, and with whom I regularly and joyously deceived her father?

'This celebration of yours?' Viola said suddenly. 'Dad has asked me to organise the food.'

'I'd rather just forget about it.'

'You can't do that. He has asked people already. He says it

will cheer you up. What about the food? Time's getting on . . . '

'Yes –'

'Dad thinks salmon? And some sort of mayonnaisy thing?'

'I am not that keen on salmon.'

'Mum, he doesn't want you to have to cook! Look, his secretary gave me this.' Viola held out a brochure. 'The partners use these people a lot.'

'Quite expensive?'

'Well, it is an important occasion,' Viola said. 'And if you *will* get married on your birthday! Actually, I agree with Dad, salmon is always popular, and you could have some chicken as well?'

How like her father she is, Jenny thought, as Viola continued to talk calmly and precisely about food, caterers, guests, who was suitable to invite, who not. Of her three children, only Simon seemed able to imagine that his mother might have interests of her own outside the family.

'Saw you in the park with one of your lovers last week, Mum,' he had said once, raising his eyebrows comically and winking.

'Oh yes? Which one?'

'That would be telling,' he said, and the conversation, light-hearted and teasing, had stopped there. But if he had caught sight of her and Iain on one of their strolls through Hyde Park, she knew that he would not be too surprised, aware perhaps that there might be areas of her life that her children were not privy to.

My real life, she thought, and remembered their meals together, the food, places where they met – country pubs, grand hotels, walking in the rain, conversations, his delight in her.

'You are such a beautiful woman. Do you know that?'

'What a flatterer,' she had replied, laughing.

'I mean it,' he said. 'I am so proud to go anywhere with you. To be seen with you, for people to think that perhaps we are connected.'

'As long as the wrong people don't see us.'

'Let them. Who cares?'

Was it that day? – when they had sat together in the out-of-the-way little French restaurant they sometimes patronised, and he had laughed and joked at her delight in choosing what she wanted to eat. At home, or whenever she accompanied her husband on one of his official occasions, she ate what was offered, what everybody else wanted or needed.

'Have something else?'

'I don't think so . . . Oh, they've got crêpes!'

'Would you like some?'

'No, really . . .'

'You would!'

'Well . . .'

'Waiter! This lady, my beautiful friend – Madam would like some of your delicious crêpes.'

And then he had watched, beaming, as she ate them. Told her again how beautiful she was, outside, inside, dressed, undressed . . .

'You make me sound like lobster!' she said. And they laughed and laughed.

After Viola had left, Jenny sat on in the garden as it cooled, an intense golden light tinged with pink staining the grass and the beds still full of autumn flowers. A robin hopped about at her feet, picking up crumbs.

An evening, a day, sometimes a day and a night for twenty-three years, she thought. Not much. How could it have gone so quickly? At the time it seemed like infinity. They often met near his work in the same quiet square, walking slowly up and down, gazing into windows, at other people's front doors, the gardens, trees and shrubs enclosed by iron railings. Then she would catch sight of him, a purposeful yet light-footed figure walking along the pavement on the other side of the square, wait for him to emerge from behind the line of parked cars, foolish smiles on both their faces.

She remembered those first meetings as an enchanted time, a magical landscape inhabited by dreams. Driving through summer lanes, woods, he had asked whether anyone knew that they were meeting that day. What was it he had said?

'One doesn't want anybody else in on something precious and beautiful like this – it would spoil everything.'

'Coward,' she said.

'Shall we stop meeting then?' And she had smiled, and taken his hand and pressed it to her lips. An unfaithful wife, she thought. Why don't I care?

She remembered a warm day in October just like this, walking together, hands clasped, arm in arm, across chalk downs, the smell of damp leaves and autumn in the air.

'Let's go back to your flat?' she had said.

'You will be late home?'

'It doesn't matter.' And careless and happy, she had sat for an hour in his car while he drove like the wind, hardly able to wait until they got back to his little mews flat.

She could hear the telephone ringing in the house, a thin thread of sound snagging on the soft evening air. It will be

John, she thought, wanting to know if Viola and she had decided on the food. The hall was dark, cool, and for a moment
she stood unmoving as the phone shrilled and screamed on the
table. But he would only ring again ten minutes later if she did
not pick up now.

'Ah, Jenny. Everything alright?'

'Fine,' she said. 'Viola was very helpful . . . We have decided
on salmon'.

The weather held. Everyone said how amazing it was for late
October – must be global warming.

'You're in luck!' Miriam said to Jenny. 'Rain is forecast, you
know!'

'Sad about Iain MacAlpine.' Miriam's husband sipped his
wine. 'I always liked him.'

'Everyone liked Iain,' Miriam said, turning to survey the
room full of people. 'Oh, there's Helen . . . On her own, poor
thing. Let's go and talk to her?'

Jenny knew that John, a good and practised speaker, would
make a speech; he always did. And towards ten o'clock he rose
to his feet. The room was crowded, groups of people standing, sitting, still eating, talking. A hush fell, and she looked
across to where he stood, a bespectacled, solid, distinguished
man, grey-haired and impeccable, speaking gracefully about
his wife of forty years, on her birthday. 'Forty happy years.
Every day . . . Well, almost every day' – laughter – 'a happy
day.' How she had been, was, the anchor, the centre of their
family, a united happy family . . . united and happy because
of her. Everyone in the room was touched as he described her
strength, unselfishness, how grateful he was for her unstinted

support all these years; always there when she was needed, calm and encouraging. How much he owed her, and how much her family – 'indeed all of us here, love her. So please, let us raise our glasses, everyone to my dear wife Jenny. Happy birthday!'

He finished, holding up his glass.

'Jenny!' echoed round the room.

Who is this person he is talking about, she thought, gazing round at the smiling faces.

Over by the window, someone started singing 'Happy Birthday', and soon the whole room had joined in. Simon pushed his way over.

'Don't look so solemn, Mum.' He laughed, putting his arms round her. 'You are meant to be enjoying this!' He looked at her plate. 'Aren't you hungry? You've hardly touched it?'

'I'm not that keen on salmon,' she said.

At midnight, the guests started to drift away, and it was after one o'clock when, the last goodbyes and congratulations said, the front door finally closed and locked, she came in from the hall.

'Well, that went off alright,' her husband said, following her in. 'A success I think? Leave those glasses, dear, the catering people and Mrs – I can never remember her name – will see to them.' He yawned. 'Splendid salmon, Jenny, an excellent choice.' He picked up some folders from a pile of documents on the table. 'Good night, my dear . . . Glad to see you enjoying yourself. Tomorrow, I need to go through all this to prepare for next week . . . A veritable mountain I'm afraid, but I suppose I will get through it.' He took off his spectacles and slipped them into the case, shutting it with a snap.

'Nice that Helen came. She seemed rather lost without Iain, I thought?' He yawned again.

'Yes . . . I won't be long,' she said. 'You go up.'

He was asleep when she finally walked upstairs, the light beside his bed still casting its pool of yellow light. She switched it off and, as her eyes adjusted, saw the outlines of the room illumined faintly by a watery, blurred-looking moon, the curtains not yet drawn. After she had undressed, she went to the window and opened it, leaning out on the sill. A few drops of rain had begun to fall, and the smell of balsam and wet grass, the night-scented stocks and phloxes planted near the house, filled the room. Below her, the garden lay grey and ghostly, dark shapes of shrubs and fruit trees patterning the pale expanse of lawn sloping away towards the patchwork of pastures and copses, woods, little villages beyond.

The rain was becoming heavier, falling softly, quietly, on the garden below, the pear tree, the long grass of the orchard, on fields and rooftops, on her home, her husband, on the grave she had never visited, on the whole long length of sleeping Britain. I might live another thirty or forty years, she thought, staring out towards the dark line of hills still just visible on the horizon. How is that possible? She got into her bed and lay, eyes open, listening to the faint rustle of water dropping through the leaves of the pear tree, her husband's quiet breathing. Thirty years, she thought again and again, gazing out into the dark. Thirty *years* . . .

The Painter

I am not clear what started me off recalling this man with such pinpoint intensity. He has not been a presence in my life for over fifty years, and even then our association was brief. What was I – eighteen, perhaps nineteen? I am in my ninth decade now. Perhaps the catalogue that arrived with a Private View card a week or two ago dislodged something? (I have always gone to his shows.) And now I am back in that world – his world: red fields, orange sky, ink-blue dark sea blotting out any ordinary vision, yet utterly convincing. Colour encompasses everything for Jon, the more so as he has become older: magical great vaulting paintings, passionate, vibrant, dazzling in their power. And they *are* powerful. Galleries in London and New York vie for his work, and all over the world people buy his paintings. I have wanted one for years, but for a long time it was financially impossible. Recently, however, and at this late stage, things seem to have changed, to my surprise. After a recent and quite unexpected windfall and almost for the first time in my life, I have real money in the bank. So why not buy one of Jon's paintings? – instead of standing looking at a blank wall imagining his violent mesmerising colour flaring across it?

The catalogue I was sent included a series of sea paintings that I have always loved; a photograph of him standing in the doorway of their beautiful house overlooking the river, and some of the house's interiors: smaller intimate paintings of children, beautiful furniture, mementoes, photographs of famous people, stacked canvases. Upstairs on the first floor, the living room with its comfortable cushioned sofas, pretty Victorian chairs and coloured rugs is, as always, suffused by that special quality of light reflected up from the surface of the river below. I haven't been in the house for years, and yet it looks quite unchanged.

I first came across Jon when, just out of the navy, he enrolled at the art school where I was a second-year student studying Art, painting in my case. He was part of an influx of recently de-mobbed men – they were mostly men – who had fought in the recent war and subsequently received grants to train as art teachers. The majority of them went on to qualify and then apply for jobs in schools. But a few used the course as a breathing space, where they could hone their skills in peace until they had, somehow, to earn a living. Jon, I knew, would continue to paint whatever happened, whether he earned a living or not.

He was a tall, monosyllabic, craggy, not particularly friendly Yorkshireman, and astonishingly talented.

'That man draws like an angel!' Rose would murmur, and it was true. His exquisite drawings of the variously posed models which confronted us reminded me very much of In-gres, or perhaps a treasured Renaissance chalk drawing, and drew admiring glances from all round the room. To me, it seemed incongruous that someone who looked as if they spent their days down the pit, or engaged in some kind of heavy manual labour, could produce drawings of such effortless skill and grace. I remember once commenting admiringly about something he was working on, and he hardly looked at me; muttering something inaudible, either embarrassed or just determined not to respond.

The end of the term was approaching. Rose was a year behind me, but we were both doing History of Art as part of our course; and although I didn't know her that well, we had decided to spend the approaching vacation hitch-hiking round Italy, soaking up Italian art. Her parents — they lived in the same beautiful house that she later inherited — seemed alarmed by their precious only daughter's travel plans. And she had to work hard to convince them that everything would be fine, that we wouldn't take unnecessary risks, would travel by train wherever feasible; that basically, it was an educational holiday. They agreed finally, gave her some money and even a grudging sort of blessing. (I could have done with a hand-out like that myself! I had been working and saving towards this holiday for months.)

That summer passed in a whirl of hot Italian days, dusty bus rides, crowded galleries and paintings — Giotto, Bellini, Botticelli, the incomparable Titian, all of them. We went to Florence and discovered Botticelli, saw Michelangelo's gigantic David; travelled to Padua and the Giotto chapel, to Siena, Verona, where we had a picnic on the amphitheatre steps. Then it was Venice. Arriving late in the evening, we walked out onto Mussolini's shallow steps leading down to the gondoliers and water taxis, immediately bewitched by the fairytale strangeness of carnival Venice at night: the masked clowns, crowds of people in fancy dress, musicians, hustlers offering us God knows what. We had booked a double room to share for the night, meaning to change to the student hostel if there was room the following day. Other students from the art school had already checked in there, Rose told me, including Jonny McClean.

I was a year ahead of Rose in terms of the course we were pursuing, so we had got to know each other only fairly recently. Of the two of us, Rose was the more sociable, easy-going one who liked to be part of a crowd; and, although we met up in the evenings, we often went our separate ways during the day. In Venice particularly, rather than joining droves of other students, I was happy to spend my time searching out the quiet squares, narrow shaded alleyways with interesting half-open doors, gardens. Best of all perhaps, the cathedral quiet of the Accademia, where I would gaze at Bellini's sublime *Madonna and Child*, pierced to the heart by Mary's calm acceptance of the horror to come.

Time passed with astonishing speed: one moment we had just arrived, and were wandering around stunned by the impossible beauty of Venice, the next we were about to leave and start on the long journey home.

I can't remember when I first noticed that Rose seemed to be talking endlessly about Jonny McClean; and that the small group of students that she went about with always included him. But then she was always more involved with the social side of things, and in Venice there had been a lot of that. By the time we had all settled down for the Christmas term it had become obvious to me, indeed to everyone, that Rose had fallen for Jonny in a big way.

'He's such a wonderful person, Katerina' – that's me – she would say. 'You should talk to him! Honestly!'

'Well I do admire his painting, Rose. Of course I do,' was all I could say.

Minor changes had taken place since the summer. Rose had moved to illustration and taken up lithography as a craft course; and Jon was now in the large painting room with me and some other Fine Art students. I saw him almost every day. He remained detached from the rest of us, only occasionally nodding his head in my direction in the morning. Sometimes when he had gone for a break I would look at what was on his easel and was always impressed. His paintings had a depth and power that gave them immense authority; the ability to convey deep emotion through colour whatever the subject matter. It was baffling. How could a switched-off block of wood paint like that?

We were over halfway through the term. At the end of a long day I was washing my brushes in the paint-encrusted sink of the grubby little wash room when Jon followed me in.

'Your painting,' he began, as I turned to look at him. 'It's good.'

'Glad you like it,' I said.

'I've seen other work of yours too.' There was a pause. 'Are you going home?' he asked.

'Yes.' I shook my brushes free of water before wrapping them in their cloth.

'Come and have a coffee,' he said. I was almost speechless with surprise. 'Or tea? We could go to Mary's,' he added – this was the run-down café near the back entrance of the art school, offering terrible coffee and soggy white bread with pies and chips, and patronised by most of the students because it was so cheap.

'Coffee's great,' I said.

For the first fifteen minutes we sat together in Mary's hardly speaking. But after a while he relaxed a little, and a creaking sort of conversation began. I discovered he had been called up at the beginning of the war, and had served as an able seaman on one of the destroyers guarding the Murmansk convoys. I had seen newsreel footage of the grim Arctic reality of those convoys, and looked at him with a new respect.

'Ninety percent boredom, ten percent fear.' He shrugged. He had always wanted to paint, he said, but there was no money; and he had left school at fifteen, destined to work in the nearby steelworks like his father.

'Saved by the war,' he said with glimmer of a smile. 'An ex-service man's grant. I wanted to show you something I have just finished.'

Half an hour more of halting conversation and I said I must go. But the ice was broken, and from now on we sometimes talked briefly in the painting room; or I would see him at Mary's or the pub, usually with the besotted Rose in tow. As I got to know him a little, I suppose my attitude changed, but not much. He was personable in a rough, road-mender sort of way, even good-looking; but it was the painting that drew me. Anyway, he belonged to Rose, didn't he?

One evening I was in one of the painting rooms rather late. I had taken a few days off because of a heavy cold and had come back to collect a canvas I was working on. I had propped it up on an easel to see where I had got to, how much more work it needed, when Jon walked into the room.

'You've been away,' he said – it was a statement rather than a question.

'I had a cold . . . Stayed at home,' I said.

'Are you better?' For once he looked at me as if he wanted to hear what I would say; stood there rocking on his heels, head on one side. 'Well, I'm glad to see you. I was afraid something had happened.'

'Like what?' I asked.

'Fallen off your bike or something?'

'I don't have a bike!' I said.

He laughed, and I laughed too – realising that I had never seen him like this before. His whole demeanour had changed, face softened and relaxed. We stood gazing at each other smiling until suddenly he stepped forward and pulled me into his arms.

'You are so beautiful,' he said, kissing me. 'And you can paint! What more can one ask?'

I was entranced of course. I was young, had not yet encountered the power and hard muscled strength of a tall young man's body. And he liked my painting! I kissed him back enthusiastically.

'What about Rose?' I asked.

'What about her?' he said, and we were still there, almost soldered together, when there was a rattle of keys and the elderly caretaker who cleaned out the painting rooms in the evenings walked in.

'Painting rooms is closed,' he said firmly. 'You shouldn't be in here at this time of night.' He held the door open very wide. 'Off you go, the two of you!'

★

At that time I was living in a small flat with my mother and two young brothers, all rather on top of each other; Jon shared a ramshackle sort of studio with four other students somewhere in south London, so privacy became a problem. Very soon, he was urging me to visit him – by which he meant move in with him, or at least for us to spend the night or part of it together. Today's youth would have succumbed before the paint was dry, so to speak. But although it was exciting to have a real man apparently in love with me, actually going off to wherever it was and sleeping in his bed odd nights amongst a crowd of students seemed somehow a step too far, and I was reluctant; content to float along in a sort of impractical romantic dream unrelated to anything, certainly not Jon.

I don't know how long this situation continued, but it was getting near Christmas and nothing ever stays the same. Sitting in Mary's late one afternoon, he said quite suddenly:

'Katerina, I want us to go away – for the night. Together. Will you come?'

'Where?' I asked.

'A nice place, a pub I know out in the country.' A student friend had recommended it. Immediately I wondered whether he had been there before with someone else – Rose, for example?

We must have taken a train, but I have no memory of it. All I remember is the small dark room, low ceiling and lace curtains, the strange unfamiliar feeling of being in a bed with a naked man: he seemed like a stranger. He made love to me in the dark, almost perfunctorily it seems to me now, although at the time I didn't know any different. In the morning, there would have been breakfast, and then a train back, I suppose? I don't remember that either.

I had a lover! I was happy, but I don't recall anything else very clearly, or what happened between us from then on – although I do remember Rose's hurt face. We must have talked together, visited galleries, discussed each other's paintings, repeated our visit to the unknown pub perhaps, but I have no memory of it. Of course, there was art school life, the other students and their various dramas, work, parties, always a lot going on. I don't remember where we were, or what we doing when I asked the age-old question: 'Do you still love me?'

There was a hiatus, a long pause while he gazed out of the window, considering. Eyes still focused beyond the window, he said: 'No . . . I don't. I don't love you.'

What happened then? Nothing. Nothing more was done, or said. Whatever it was that had existed between us flapped off into the night, defeated. The term ended, another began. Life went on. I don't remember being particularly unhappy, although I think my pride was hurt. But then I won a prize for a painting I had submitted to an inter-art-schools competition, and my attention shifted to other things.

After a very short time, Jon went back to Rose. I don't know whether she knew about me and Jon or not. Anyway, a few months later, Rose told me that she and Jon were getting married. And they did – I went to their wedding. It was a huge affair – Jon looked magnificent rather than happy in his bridegroom's outfit, and I could see at once that he had moved up in the world. Some of the other guests seemed way above me or my family on the social scale, and I spotted at least one bishop in the distance, fat gold cross gleaming on his purple chest. I looked around for any students from the art school and saw one or two familiar faces, but not many. Standing in a corner clutching my champagne, I overheard one of the impeccably dressed guests remark to another: 'Bit of a rough diamond, this painter fella? Let's hope he treats our little Rose decently, eh?'

This was about the time I learned about the beautiful family house on the river, the parents wanting to move to a smaller place in the country – I had to laugh when I heard that. No need for the 'rough diamond' to take up a part-time teaching job then, I thought, all is well. And from then on, gradually we went our separate ways. I would get news of them from time to time, often at someone else's private view. We exchanged Christmas cards – or rather, Rose and I did, and I always received invitations to his exhibitions. Mostly I skipped the openings, and went the following week instead. Years ago and before Jon became known, I gave my youngest son one of his smaller paintings as a wedding present. In retrospect I think he would have preferred something more practical. But that was then and this is now, I thought. It is my turn now and this is the moment.

It is remarkably easy to acquire a work of art if you know what you want and have the money – and this transaction was simplicity itself. I knew exactly which painting it was to be, one of the majestic and beautiful sea paintings that I have always loved. Jon's gallery proved very helpful, and it all went ahead without a hitch; the money was paid, arrangements made, insurance in place, and Jon's painting arrived at my front door. The whole house felt like a different place with the arrival of this one painting. The atmosphere it created was extraordinary. I felt different too, and spent hours just leaning against the wall opposite, taking it in, knowing that in a million years I would never tire of it.

It had been a long time since I had been in touch with Jon – or Rose either, for that matter – and once the painting was up on the wall, I wanted to tell him. At first, I thought I would email him. But then, as I didn't seem to have an up-to-date email address, I wrote a short letter instead.

Dear Jon,

I don't know if the gallery has mentioned it to you, but I am now the proud owner of your Sea Painting no. 5. I have hung it – I hope in the right place, and it looks wonderful. Perhaps you will come and see for yourself? I love this particular painting, and look at it every day. I'll never tire of it.

Hope you are well and flourishing.

All love,

Katerina

After it had been posted, I regretted sending a letter. Emails are so much more immediate; and I knew from experience that Jon was not a natural communicator and if he commented at all, it would only be after a long wait. In fact, if I heard anything it would probably be through Rose. So when a few weeks later Rose telephoned, I was half expecting it.

'Hello! Lovely to hear you, Rose . . . You know I have bought a painting of Jon's?'

'Yes –'

'It's up on the wall! Looks wonderful! How are you both?'

'Katerina –'

'I wrote to him, to tell him – '

'Yes – '

'Has he read my letter? I wanted to thank him.'

'Yes, your letter . . . I don't know.' She stopped speaking and a silence ensued which lasted so long I thought the line had become disconnected.

'Rose?'

'I did give it to him, but I don't think he – '

'What? . . . Has something happened?'

'A short illness . . .' Her voice trailed off again.

'What do you mean? He's OK, isn't he?'

'No, Katerina, I – I . . .'

'Rose, what's happened?'

'Jon died . . . Last week, a stroke.'

It was my turn to be lost for words. But I have to admit that while it was a shock to hear that he had died, of course, the first thought that came into my mind was that he had not read my letter. So he didn't know that I had bought a painting of his and how much I admired and loved it? For some reason, this has upset me far more than the fact that he has died.

Birthdays

Before he left for his conference, Jane Wilmot's husband reminded her again about the steak.

'Don't forget this.' He held the fridge door open, pointing.

'It's only Friday.'

'Shouldn't be wasted. Expensive stuff nowadays.'

Jane sat drinking her tea silently, wishing he would go. She hated breakfast; today was worse. I should know better, she thought, by now.

'I had a dream last night,' her husband said suddenly. 'Yes.' He studied the empty square of window between them speculatively. 'Dreamed I emptied this place out, tidied it up . . .' He waved a hand towards the trailing profusion of pot plants, magazines, her pink lustre jugs, sewing basket on the broad sill, books on the end of the table. 'All this . . . rubbish, bits everywhere. Just cleared it out. And the boy's things all over the house. Junk. By the way' – he put down his cup – 'when does the university term end? I suppose Mathew will be home soon? You realise I can't stay in the house with him. Last holiday nearly killed me. That music!'

'Yes.'

'I shall stay in the flat at the office. Or at Gerald's. Better for everyone.'

'Yes.'

Certainly better for Mathew, if he ever came home again. Flat at the office – she knew what that meant. Alice. She wondered if the conference was Alice too; or maybe Gerald? She was never sure. It might be either – or both.

'I must be off. I'm late. Where are my gloves?'

'In the hall, on the shelf.' Where they have been for the last eighteen years, she thought; the last eighteen hundred thousand years.

He took an apple from the fruit bowl under the window, holding it up to the light to inspect it for blemishes, cleanliness, stood fidgeting with the conference papers; middle-aged, balding, a neat compact man, too glossy somehow, like his case of fine black leather. By accident, she had once come across the bill for it in a coat pocket and could hardly believe that it was possible to buy a briefcase for that amount of money. She brushed the crumbs that lay round her plate into a small inexact pyramid, remembering other things she had found in his pockets, also by accident.

'I didn't sleep well last night,' he said without looking at her. 'Must have been that cheese thing you made.'

'Fish.'

'What?'

'Fish, not cheese.'

He glanced at her briefly out of eyes like hard little berries: unripe, black, sharp, at odds with the soft pinkness of his face. Jane moved the crumb pyramid into another position.

'Oh!' He folded his newspaper into careful knife-edge folds. 'Well, whatever it was gave me indigestion. And that dream.'

Jane did not reply. From the hall she heard him call out, 'You haven't forgotten? About next week?' Next week, when was that? It seemed an unimaginable distance away.

'Monday. The overseas director and his wife . . .' She missed the end of the sentence, then he was back in the kitchen leafing through the morning's mail.

'Try and get the house decent, dear, will you? These should be cleaned.' A scarf and a woollen cardigan were laid beside her plate. 'It's an extremely important contact, particularly as the chairman will be here too . . . He should have the grey room, view over the garden. Things must go smoothly, Jane, look good. The guest rooms – ' He broke off, handed her a square stiff envelope. 'Letter for you. Mrs Harris should do it; she's paid enough. And Jane – ' He was standing directly before her, balancing his polished case full of papers, minutes, notes, company law, on the table. 'Jane! Are you listening?' She could have said something then, but she didn't. If only he would go.

'Could you see that there are flowers this time? A really nice arrangement in the hall? Get some from that florist woman in the square, flowers make such a difference. Now, must go. I shall be late.' He patted her on the shoulder hurriedly. Like a dog, she thought, a faithful stupid dog. 'Don't forget the meat!'

The front door banged as it did every morning, except today she had half-expected something different, and now the whole weekend stretching ahead. Was it Monday or Tuesday he had said they were coming? She couldn't remember. Outside, the car started up and moved away, crackling over the frozen gravel and ice on the drive. A faint murmur from the engine sounded in the kitchen for a while, then faded, and silence returned. A silence so absolute that she could hear her own heart beating out its neat tidy rhythm, lightly, methodically, as if it cared for nothing except itself.

'Bloody nothing!' she shouted suddenly and picked up the envelope, its contents already clear in her mind.

'To the Best Mum!' was scrawled across the card. 'Happy Birthday. For Ever and Ever. LuvYer. Matt.' At the bottom he had pencilled in a row of large untidy kisses.

After she had seen the milkman, stacked the breakfast things, she took her card and walked slowly up the wide stairs to stand by the window of one of the big empty rooms on the first floor.

The snow stretched like a soiled counterpane across the drive and lawns, the orchard, and beyond that the farm, grey fields folded down to the valley. She always knew when John was lying by his sudden concern, reasonableness, the way he smiled at her. Probably this time it *was* a conference. Absently she picked at the hardened skin round her nails. She should have done something: cut them, shaped them, removed the ragged cuticle. But she hadn't bothered. Too much hardened skin, or something of the kind; pitted brown freckles on her hands, liver going to pieces, aching bones. The doctor had said at your age you must expect these things. But she knew it wasn't just age – although it makes no difference now, she thought, turning from the window.

Why was she always so cold? Of course the heating in this great mausoleum was set to turn down in the day. Economy, in spite of the new car. When he was little, Matt had once asked her whether they were rich or poor, and to her surprise she had been unable to answer him. Absurd really. She would know what to say now.

It was just as cold downstairs, colder. In the hall her breath hung on the air, small wreaths of vapour. She decided to take out the bottle of wine she had been hiding under the coats at the back of the downstairs cloakroom. She had stolen it deliberately, a few weeks ago, from the local supermarket. Dark, inviting, a large bottle of expensive red wine, it had stood waiting on the further side of her mountain of shopping, left behind by the woman in front. Nobody had noticed when, without hesitating, Jane had picked it up and put it in one of her own baskets.

She switched on the television, wrapped herself up in a duvet just cleaned for one of the guest rooms and leaned back on the sofa. It gave her an obscure satisfaction to be drinking stolen wine. She sighed and drank deeply, the wine flooding through her like new warm blood. The television flickered into life and a woman's face filled the square pale void and hung there disembodied, talking silently. It was obvious that she was thinking as she talked, considering her words slowly, with care; that she felt deeply, intensely about whatever was under discussion. Jane poured herself out more wine and turned up the sound.

'. . . a kind of honesty between two people. One of the happiest marriages. I shall never forget it. My cousin . . .'

Onto the screen came the image of another face, bone-thin, delicate, sad; mouth childish and soft below the glittering eyes. Jane sat up, startled, recognising her neighbour, Camilla, the writer who for years had lived with her husband on the farther side of the orchard. Famous – or famous now: there was an exhibition of her books permanently on show at the local library. The children, Mathew in particular, had heard all about her and were impressed that their mother had once known, even talked to her.

'. . . they understood each other perfectly. A wonderful partnership. Unconventional, but then they were unconventional people and of course he protected her – he had to. What time to go to bed, when to leave the party, whether a particular guest would upset her, all her money affairs. She was tremendously vulnerable, sensitive . . .'

Blinded by the past, Jane gazed at the television. Louis and Camilla! Their faces were so clear in her mind, they could be sitting opposite; and yet it must be years, years! Of the two it had been Louis she had known best, Louis that she remembered best. She wondered if he were still alive; he had seemed old then. Above the glass-topped table the television repeated 'Never forget, never forget' like a litany, but it was the voice from the past which she heard: calm, ironic, considered, rather high for a man. Louis's voice.

'My wife? Ah, Jane, I am lucky if I catch sight of her myself. So little time, so very little time for us poor mortals,' and, laughing, he would make some wry comment about his role as a 'kept man', as he put it.

Louis suffered from poor health and never went to any job as far as she knew, never had – although someone once told her that he wrote too. She had never seen him writing or indeed doing anything much, except sit by the fire reading. It had never struck her as in any way odd at the time.

'Camilla?' he would say if asked about his wife. 'Oh, Camilla has more important things to do than talk to us. She is a writer.'

It was said with such a gentle smile, a kindly humorous

expression lighting up the large grey eyes, that Jane, disarmed, had dismissed the sudden intuition that the word had been intended as an insult, as if he had said 'whore' or 'thief'. But then Louis was disarming. Doubts vanished when he smiled, talked. Tall and slender, with thin attenuated fingers and a deliberate courteous manner, he was an attractive man: witty, well informed, with unusual views on almost everything. Jane enjoyed talking to him – and walking through the long grass to the little gate in the hedge, perhaps to bring a letter wrongly delivered, lettuces when there were too many, apples in the autumn, or merely for company – and always hoped it would be Louis she would see, not Camilla. If Camilla did appear, as likely as not he would say, 'Ah! You are here, dear. Thought you were hard at work. I told Jane you were too busy to see anyone.' And Camilla would smile her haunting, haunted smile, enquire whether Annie, their help, had brought him tea or coffee, what he was reading, what time they should have lunch, before slipping away across the grass to that dog-kennel place of hers – the summer house, they called it.

Even now, visiting Americans and everyone else always exclaimed when they saw that, with its view of the pond, the woods crowding down the slopes of the far-off hazy valley; secluded yet intimate, enclosed yet open to the spaces of the world – her world, thought Jane, glass empty against her cheek. How had he managed it? To trap and tame such a wild spirit? Although it was only much later, when she had read Camilla's books, from curiosity more than anything else, that Jane understood what manner of woman had lived in the little cottage behind the hedge for all those years. At the time

Camilla's silence seemed impenetrable. Louis was the hospitable, affable neighbour, his wife merely a shadowy figure forever flitting out to her refuge in the garden.

'I am of course fortunate to be married to such a talented woman,' he once remarked to Jane. 'It's difficult for her since my health . . . I am a bit of a broken reed these days.' And, whispering, he had added, 'But then she is happier working on her books. Must be kept busy. No time to, to . . .' He left the sentence unfinished. Time? – for what? The room with its thick cottage walls, uneven boards, seemed airless, momentarily heavy with something she could not define; and the rugs, daffodils made brilliant by bands of spring sunshine, even the living flame of the wood fire before which they sat, did nothing to dispel the feeling of time suspended, objects and people caught within its flux like flies on a flypaper. Then came the day of the raspberries.

Jane had woken early, alone, and as it was fine and warm and for some reason the children were not yet awake, had gone out into the garden to pick raspberries. It was a good year and, filling a large bowl before she had realised how many more there were to come, she decided to take some across to Camilla and Louis: he not fit enough to care for their overgrown vegetable patch, she unable to spare the time.

As Jane walked along the brick path towards the cottage, its windows open to the morning sun, she heard Louis speaking. The venom and fury in his voice astonished, horrified her, and she halted abruptly.

'– have what you want! How nice. Wouldn't we all! Where is that wonderful imagination we are always hearing so much about? Can't you imagine that I might wish things to be different too? Very different, actually. But such privileges of choice are only open to the fortunate – to you, it appears. Naturally.'

'But Louis' – Camilla's reply was hesitant, trembling, desperate. Jane knew she was on the edge of tears. 'Louis, why not? I am not too old. The doctor –'

'That doctor is an irresponsible fool!'

Silence, and Jane felt her fingers grow clammy on the bowl held rigidly before her. Louis spoke again:

'You can barely cope now. How on earth do you think you would manage?' Camilla did not reply and Louis laughed quietly. 'You! – of all people. With a baby!'

Eavesdropping on the path, Jane was stunned. A baby? – Camilla and Louis?

But they were so old. The idea seemed perverse, indecent almost.

'Let's be honest, Camilla,' Louis continued while Jane waited. 'Let us at least attempt a little honesty for once. You know how you feel, how you are, about your work. Being disturbed. Think of Jane Wilmot's children – how they . . . upset you.'

'They don't! I like them – it's you they upset. Anyway, that's different. If it were my own –'

'You are being unrealistic, ridiculous. An invalid husband and a child? It's bad enough as it is. How do you think it would be for me? The extra burden? I realise it is difficult for you, although God knows I do what I can.' His voice was calm, clear, strong. 'I am not ill for amusement, you know. Does that occur to you?'

Camilla's whispered reply was almost inaudible. If Jane had

not been standing directly beside the window she would have missed it.

'The doctor says, they all say – that you, that there is nothing wrong. That –'

'I know what they say. Not very original of them. And your marvellous doctor, what does he think we should do for money? Have you asked him that? How do you think we would manage?'

'Louis, I want a baby. Soon I will be too old. We'll manage somehow, people do. I can go on working, but I – I – want a baby of my own!' This came out as a muted groan, as if Camilla had sunk down on the floor, unable to bear the weight of her anguish. Unable to bear anything at all, thought Jane, except words.

There was a pause, a painful cessation of speech, silence, and Jane knew suddenly that this scene had been enacted many times before, probably over years. At last Louis's voice came from the window.

'My dear, before you get hysterical, why not go out to the summer house and try to do some work? That will make you feel – calmer. When Annie comes, I will ask her to bring you some coffee.' The cool triumph in his voice was unimaginably shocking. Taking care not to make a sound, Jane set down the bowl of raspberries and ran.

During her few visits in the months that followed, this unseen drama was always present in her mind – although she could detect no changes, no cracks in the outward minutiae of the life that continued apparently unruffled, beyond the apple trees: Louis wrapped in his rug in the living room, his wife working on the 'new book'.

Then, early one Sunday morning, a few weeks before Christmas, Camilla was found in the beech wood below the cottage. Bare-footed and in a thin cotton nightdress, she had run out into the snow, poured petrol over herself and set it alight.

Until then, Jane had been unaware of what a well-known, well-thought-of figure her neighbour had been. With Camilla's death and the manner of it, this changed. It was headline news and articles, reminiscences, appreciations continued to flood the newspapers for weeks, if not months, and Jane read everything she could find. Books were written about Camilla; and the village, more interested in her dead than alive, gossiped voraciously. Louis moved away and for a time Jane heard nothing of him, nor did she wish to. But, as custodian of his wife's fame, he was in demand; indeed, he was an authority, *the* authority. After a decent interval, as Jane thought of it, and supported by not inconsiderable royalties, gradually he emerged – to become a celebrity, a part he played to perfection.

He was doing it now. Jane leaned forward, spilling her wine. There he sat before her on the screen, older, more lined, desiccated, the flesh on his already thin face hanging in folds but talking, as he always had, calmly and with complete assurance.

'My wife was an immensely talented woman, happy in her talent. It was a great privilege to care for her,' he said with conviction, staring apparently straight into Jane's eyes. 'Of course, she suffered, suffered greatly; she had an unduly sensitive and vulnerable nature. But her genius as a writer – '

Happy? *Happy?* She was crazy, mad! You drove her crazy,

Jane thought, and saw again the red glow of Camilla's blind behind the trees of the orchard at two, three, four in the morning. She, Jane, had been woken by one of the children, but what was Camilla doing up at that time of night in the summer house? Writing? Unable to stay, unable to go, in the end . . . So much for honesty. Jane was surprised to find that there were tears in her eyes. Someone was talking again.

'. . . to remember this woman, a writer of such distinction and courage who died on her birthday fifteen years ago . . .'

Jane got up quickly and switched off the television. She had forgotten about the birthday. Clutching the duvet to her, she stood in the centre of the cold silent room trembling and weeping. It's the wine, she thought; gone to my head. But as she stood there, staring out at the darkening sky above the snow-bright trees, she knew it wasn't the wine. And when at last she put down her glass and spoke on the telephone, it was calmly and quite deliberately. Like Louis.

They came early, but she was ready. There was not much difficulty except for the photograph albums. Kneeling on the study floor she had wavered for a moment; then remembered when the children were small and there had still seemed some sort of hope and promise: the girls on the beach, picking flowers in the orchard, in plays at school, and so much later Matt, the only creature in the world she loved wholeheartedly, with passion, ecstasy almost. It was wrong, she knew, to love sons like that.

From the open pages of the album his young shining blazing face smiled up at her, untried, unvanquished. She remembered her husband's dream.

'All this!' She handed the albums to one of the men, gestured towards the stack of cardboard boxes, furniture, books, bundles heaped together in the centre of the kitchen. 'To go.'

'And the lounge, madam? China cabinet, silver trophies and that?'

'To be left.' The furniture van was parked outside the front door – who had noticed its arrival and departure? She had made sure it carried no address. One thing at a time, she thought. I can move it all on to another store tomorrow.

The hall seemed even colder, naked without its familiar clutter: Mathew's old bicycle, the outgrown boots, anoraks, woolly hats, old gloves, her gardening basket. In the downstairs cloakroom only John's things and one of her own coats remained. She draped it round her shoulders and walked through into the kitchen. It too was almost empty – except for the spotless units, machines, copper saucepans, Mrs Harris's pride and joy. The jars of herbs, tattered cookery books, fruitwood chairs had all gone, packed up with her bundles of dried flowers and the old brown dresser, its crockery now in orderly piles behind closed and shining cupboard doors. Even the marks where chairs had scuffed and scraped for so many years had all but been obliterated, scrubbed clean when she washed the floor.

Slowly she went through the house, checking each room. Like unravelled stitches, holes in the fabric gaped at her. The portrait of her as a child, the green velvet upholstered chair inherited from her mother; the quilt – how many years had that taken? – the rush-topped stool Matt had made for her at school; small mementos on the mantelpiece, stones, shells collected on holiday; books, random messages scribbled on telephone books, out-of-date shopping reminders: in each room her absence was palpable.

Closing the front door, she pushed the key through the letter box and heard it rattle on the polished tiles within. Nothing left of her at all now – except the key, and the flowers in the hall. A florist's perfect meaningless arrangement.

Large irregular flakes of snow were falling again. For a moment she stood looking up at it drifting down on her, white, heavy, like a pall, a shroud, the end of the world, and an image of frantic footsteps beneath beech trees came into her mind. She picked up her bag with her night things and, stepping into the snow, walked quickly along the drive towards the lane. Behind her in the gleaming empty kitchen the oven, set on a timer, switched itself on and began to hum. So as not to waste it she had left the steak in two glasses of red wine to cook slowly and gently, ready just about the time John was due home. For dinner, late on Monday, he had said. His birthday.

Mountain Bike Unit

The boys were fighting again. Although she was a floor below, Eve could hear them thumping about, screeching and bellowing at each other. Someone is going to get really hurt one day, she thought, putting Louisa back in her carrying chair and getting up from the table. There was a crash as a door upstairs was slammed violently shut, and then Sammy on the staircase, shrieking: 'I hate you! I HATE you!'

Standing in the kitchen doorway, she called up to him. 'Sammy? . . . Sammy!'

He stamped down the stairs, sobbing with hurt pride and fury, burrowed into her stomach, flailing arms sending her mug of coffee sideways across the kitchen table and onto the floor.

'*Sammy!* Calm down. That might have gone all over Louisa!'

'I don't CARE! He – he – doesn't let me play –'

'Well, leave him alone, then.' She found a cloth – filthy, God knows where that had been – and started mopping up.

'I *hate* him!' A bruise was beginning to swell at the side of his forehead, and his face was tear-stained and red.

'No, you don't. Here, come and talk to me.' She pulled the tense, heaving little body against her own soft bulk, stroked his hair gently. 'Just let him be, darling. Max is – is . . . He

likes to be on his own sometimes.' (Shut away, off in his own
world that he doesn't want to share, she thought.) 'Come on,
cheer up. Dad's coming home early for a half-term treat today. He's taking you both to the zoo.'

'Not with *him!* Pig!'

'He's taking you both,' Eve said sighing.

PRIVIT
Keep Out!!
On pane of DEATH

Max read the notice he had pinned up on his door and slammed
it shut again. Still in his dark green pyjamas – although his
mother had told him to get dressed an hour ago – he stood
stiffly to attention as he always did when summoning his
troops. The roll call first, then he would address the men, inform them of his plans for the day. He scanned the eager, res-
olute faces waiting for his command.

'Good morning, men. The situation is dangerous, but not
one that is beyond us. The enemy is strong and there is a great
need for –' He couldn't think of the word – care, trouble?
Neither was right. 'In a moment we will carry out our drill
as usual, but after that we will be doing something different. Please listen carefully, as I am going to tell you about
today's special manoeuvres. Even though we are top fighting
men of the famous Mountain Bike Unit, you will need extra
training for this, and at eleven hundred hours exactly we will
leave on a new exercise. But before we start –' He broke off,
suddenly remembering the word he wanted. 'Vigilance,' he
said firmly. 'All the time, we must remember –'

The door opened and his younger brother stood there again, this time eating a piece of toast and dripping honey down the front of his jersey.

'Mum says are you dressed yet?'

It was not permitted for a Mountain Bike officer to show emotion before his men, one had to lead by example. So he contented himself with a stony glare, and a quiet 'Get out of my room, turd-face.'

'You're playing soldiers, aren't you?'

'Get out!'

'Baby!'

Max stared impassively towards the sticky smiling face, remembering just in time to dismiss his men: it was important and a matter of pride never to mix the life of the Mountain Bike Unit with the messy details of his everyday family life. Then he was out in the passage and chasing after Sammy, shouting angrily. Max had the bigger room now because he was the older one and had homework to do, and anyway his mother thought that perhaps they would get on better if they were separated.

'Ba-by, ba-by,' chanted Sammy.

Instead of bolting into his own room, Sammy made for the bathroom and then locked it, refusing to come out even when Max threatened to smash the door down. He kicked at the door, but in his flimsy bedroom slippers only stubbed his toes. Of course, if he hadn't dismissed the men, they could have brought up heavy artillery and finished the job he thought. No problem. He walked back along the passage to his brother's bedroom.

Close up under the eaves, the room had an attractive cosy

feel. A yellow teddy bear leaned back against the pillows, and a new duvet cover that Sam had chosen himself – red, his favourite colour – covered the bed in fiery glowing folds. T-shirts and vests, pants just out of the dryer, had been stacked in a neat pile on the chair. Mum had made the bed, so of course it all looked tidy. It was so unfair. Because he was three years older, Max was supposed to make his own bed *and* do Saturday morning chores *and* he had homework. He stood listening to Sammy shouting something in the bathroom. How was it that nobody except him could see what he was really like? Always *there* for a start, spoiling everything, and Mum always on his side. Nothing good about him at all, little turd. He, Max, had been promised a proper mountain bike to replace the old one, but who gets the new bike at Christmas? Fat-face of course. And just because he was worried about his stupid job, Dad had given *him* all that crap about enjoying what he'd got, things are tight, old chap, money doesn't grow on trees, blah, blah, blah! He leaned forward against the chair to watch a tractor turn out of the farm, and a red T-shirt slid off the pile onto the floor. He glared angrily at it for a moment and then picked it up and threw it out of the open window. Looking down, he could see it lying in a satisfactorily crumpled heap on the gravel. He picked up the bear and the pillows, the pile of clothes, and chucked them out; then, intoxicated, dragged the duvet off the bed – quite big and heavy – and pushed that over the sill as well. He was looking round for something else when his mother came in to the room.

'Max? Are you dressed yet? What are you doing? *Max!* That's all just been ironed! What the hell? My God, you are –' And she slapped him, hard, on the thigh and again on the leg.

Max stared at his leg for a moment, and then walked past her and down the stairs, straight out of the house. Down the path to the white gate which separated the front garden and its big apple tree from the lane, past the farm and its mucky yard, loping quickly along the rough unmade road towards the church and the village beyond.

'Max, *Max*! Come back! *MAX!* Do you hear me?'

Eve leaned out of the window, watching him. He is in his pyjamas, she thought, let him go. It won't be far. She extricated Sammy from the bathroom – the lock had jammed again – and picked up Louisa, who was gripping the sides of her carrying chair, making strenuous efforts to pull herself upright while screaming the house down. She'll be out of there soon, she thought, and then it really will be a madhouse. Oh God, I shouldn't have hit him. What's the matter with me? I've never done that before. She went to the window to look down the lane. He'll soon be back, she thought. Anyway, where can he go?

She was making scrambled eggs and burning the toast for the second time when she heard Donald's car. Thank heavens! It was two and a half hours since Max had walked out of the house, and he had not returned. She had been down the lane as far as the village shop, had asked everybody but no one had seen him. She was beginning to feel panicky, tearful.

'It's all my fault, Donald . . . But I am so tired.' (What a lame excuse. How could she? Hit her own child, her own darling Max?) 'I – I just lost it . . . Oh God, I'll never forgive myself if – if – '

'That boy! What's got into him?'

Donald threw his paper onto the table, frowning. Always trouble, he thought. He hadn't realised that children would be like this . . . continual drama. Winding everybody up until they snapped – it was considerably more peaceful at the office. 'Eve! You're over-reacting. Come on.' He put his arms round her. 'He's just gone off in a strop, the little so-and-so. Eve! Stop it! I won't have you upset like this –'

'Supposing he doesn't come back?'

'Of course he will. But better ring round and see if he's gone to Billy's mum, or –'

'They are away for half term.'

'What about Tom and Margaret?'

'Done that already'

And he's not hiding in the garden, or the orchard?'

Holding Louisa and with Sammy trailing after them disconsolately – 'When are we going to the zoo Daddy? When are we . . .?' – they went out of the back door and walked to the fence which marked the boundary between their ragged country garden, the orchard belonging to the farm and the fields beyond. Not a sign of Max, or anyone else for that matter. Eve felt sick, and Donald fumed and snorted.

'That boy! I'll give him something to remember –'

'You going for him too won't help. It's my fault, Donald!'

'Oh rubbish! He's just –'

'There's a reason – I should have played it differently. How can he stay out like this? Where's he *gone?*' She put her head in her hands, sobbing.

'Eve! For God's sake, stop crying. He's got to learn not to do this sort of thing. Anyway, he shouldn't have chucked all those things out of the window. That's completely out of

order. We – are – not – going – to – the – zoo – Sammy.'
Donald enunciated this sentence with exaggerated precision,
and she knew that he was beginning to lose it too. '*Why?* Because your brother has run off and not told us where he was
going. So we bloody have to look for him, don't we?'

'I'll help you,' Sammy said. 'He is *bad*, isn't he, Mummy?'

At three they rang the police.

Max had not continued along the road but turned in at the
gate which led to the farm, walked across the lawn at the
front and past the Virginia creeper that covered the house,
climbed over the wall at the back and then dropped down
into the field on the far side. From here, although at a distance
and partly obscured by the trees of the orchard, he had a view
of the back windows of the cottage, indeed the windows of
his own room. He stood looking at them, wishing that he
had got his army binoculars with him. Nothing seemed to
be happening, no one had come out looking for him. They
didn't care, that was the truth. They didn't care and nor did
he. He was an officer of the famous Mountain Bike Unit,
brave as a lion, and his men would follow him to the ends of
the earth. He cleared his throat and put his arms down by his
sides stiffly – he always did this when he was about to address
the men.

'Fall in, men. We're on our own now. The unit will proceed
to . . . to higher ground where – where we will be in a better position'. He looked up at the outlines of the beech woods
reaching down towards the flat farmland. The fresh green
fluttering leaves hung down above the edges of the field, deep
shadow beneath. He longed to get up there. Anywhere away

from this – this – place, my 'home', he thought, rage surging through him again.

Arriving at the far edge of the field, he gave the order to disperse and, holding his rifle at the ready, led the way under the barbed-wire fence and up the crumbling chalk path between the first towering beech trees. Very quickly, the path became almost vertical and then changed direction, turning into a narrow beaten track traversing the steep hillside, wild yew and scrub between the trees falling away below in a dense wild jungle. Scratchy streamers of bramble reached towards him, tearing at his legs, and the clay and moss made it slippery and hard going in places. Scrambling onto a colossal uprooted tree that had fallen across the path, he stood for a moment looking down across the valley. Over the tops of the trees below, he could see right down and across the village, pick out the church tower, the little grey ribbon of road twisting down to the shop. Last week when he and his father had come up to the woods, without Sammy for once, Dad had shown him how to grab hold of one of the long tough creepers that hung down from the beeches here and swing himself out into space and back like a commando. But that was last week. He was never going back there again, *ever*.

At the top of the beech hangar the path led onto a wide level gated avenue, carpeted with last year's leaves, cool and green in the hottest summers. Beyond it, and just visible through the trees, picnic tables were set up for walkers and people who drove up here on the forestry road at weekends.

For half an hour, Max drilled his men: formed squares, marched them in close formation, practised approaching the enemy unseen and, most important of all, instructed them on the care and use of the new Mountain Bikes. These were the best machines that money could buy; and the men who rode them, the best men. Heroes, we are heroes, he thought.

'Shoulder *arms!*' He smiled at them. 'We're making good progress. Mountain bike manoeuvres next. Move on, men . . .'

Donald was talking to the police on the telephone.

'. . . nine, nearly ten, small for his age. What? On the edge of the village . . . The cottage backs onto farmland. Yes, a number of outbuildings . . . We're next to the farm. Wells? Oh, you mean? . . . I don't know. What?' He held up his hand as Eve whispered something.

'Tell them he's been gone since eleven o'clock!'

'Hang on, you better speak to my wife.' He leaned over and handed Eve the phone. 'They want to know what he was – *is* – wearing?'

'Dark green pyjamas, Marks and Spencer,' Eve said, hardly able to speak. 'Bedroom slippers – or maybe trainers?'

'Try not to worry, madam, boys of his age often do this.' Had there been some sort of – well, disagreement? A row? Or anything like that? the policeman asked.

'I lost my temper . . . He had thrown all his brother's bed clothes out of the window, you see.' How ridiculous and petty that sounded. Why on earth should she have reacted like she did? What sort of mother . . . The wailing commentary in her head started up again.

The policeman interrupted. 'They know how to rile their mothers alright, I've got a boy myself.' For a moment she thought he was going to start telling her about problems with his own son. 'We'll alert the road patrols, give them a description,' he continued calmly. 'If he doesn't turn up pretty soon, we'll get his details circulated, make enquiries via the motorway police, lorry drivers . . . Did you say he had blond hair?'

'Brown hair . . . In his pyjamas,' Eve said faintly, handing the phone back to Donald.

When he had hung up, Donald said, 'They are going to send an officer round. Do a search of the farm outbuildings, see if there are any wells there.'

'Wells?' Eve looked at him aghast, and they gazed at each other silently.

'Probably he's fallen down a well!' Sammy said. 'Then he won't *ever* come back, will he?'

'Don't say things like that!' Donald sounded shocked, and Eve knew he was thinking – little monster! What's happened, why are my children like this? 'Of course he's coming back!'

'When?'

'Later. Go and fetch my case from the hall . . . please.'

'What if he – he doesn't . . . come back, Donald? What are we going to do?' Eve whispered as Sammy went off to look for the case.

'He will.' He put an arm round her shoulders. 'Has he got his mobile with him?'

'He was in his pyjamas, Donald!'

'Have you looked?'

'Yes.'

'Don't worry. He'll come back.' But she could sense that he was less confident.

★

A number of parking and picnic areas had been built across the beech woods, and he was walking along the edge of the first of them now. At one of the wooden tables a couple had just sat down and were opening a rucksack. Glancing at them cursorily as he passed, Max realised suddenly that he was extremely hungry.

'Hello,' the man said, staring at him rather hard. 'Enjoying a day in the woods?' Max nodded, made to walk on. He could smell the potato crisps the woman was opening. Smoky bacon, his favourite.

'All alone?'

'I – I am meeting – some, some friends up here.'

'A rendezvous?'

'But they haven't turned up yet,' Max continued, standing first on one leg then the other.

'I expect they will,' the man said. 'What time were you meeting them?'

Max gazed at him blankly – nosy or what? He had no idea what the time was anyway, so whatever he said would sound peculiar. Not that it had anything to do with this geezer.

'Have a biscuit?' the man said.

'Thanks. I'll have to walk back if they don't come soon.'

'Where do you live, then?'

Max waved airily towards the trees behind him. 'Not far. Down there. We often come up here.'

'Why are you wearing pyjamas?' the woman asked.

Max hesitated for a moment as he ate another biscuit 'Doing it for a bet,' he said. 'I think I'll start back now . . .'

'Perhaps we could give you a lift?'

'No thanks. I am not allowed to take lifts . . . I'll just walk on – to – the next car park at Green Hollow,' he said, turning towards the broad forestry road, flinty surface shining in the sun. 'Probably they are waiting there'.

The Green Hollow picnic area was in a quieter, more distant section of the woods on the further side of the hangar, and the men had orders to reassemble at a spot he and his friend Jack had found just below the forestry road. Secluded and yet accessible, it was as if someone had scooped a giant shallow bowl out of the hillside, perfect for someone on a bike to ride round its rim, pause for a moment, then swoop down into the hollow and out again very quickly, finishing up with a wheelie, or spin, or something spectacular, on the opposite edge. Exactly the right sort of place for Mountain Bike manoeuvres, he thought. Nobody could see him, interrupt him, *interfere* with anything here.

It was very quiet, nobody about in this stretch of the woods. All he could hear were the birds whistling and singing, the beech leaves crackling under his feet. He knew it well from all the dreary family walks up here: Sammy moaning on about something boring, Dad talking to Mum with his cross don't-interrupt-me face on. (He was always cross actually, not just on walks, all the time.) My *family*, he thought bitterly.

A hundred yards or so further on from the hollow, the main forestry road divided, and another narrower track led down to the small town where his mother did her shopping, they all went to the dentist, and where Jack lived. Apart from his men, Jack was the only person in the world who understood about Sammy. And Jack's mother was nice too. She never bothered about boots off at the front door, tidy rooms, homework and that sort of thing. He decided that after the manoeuvres, he would walk on down to Jack's. His mum would be sure to give him something to eat if he turned up out of the blue. She was like that.

There was one small van in the parking area when he got to it, otherwise it was deserted. Someone had been there, however, as on one of the wooden tables he saw some plastic beakers and other litter, and an almost full sandwich carton. Cheese, just what he liked. Munching bread and cheese, he started off down the track towards the Hollow. Then he saw the man.

At first he hardly noticed him, and walked on scuffing his feet through the beech leaves, and listening to the birds. Then something made him look round. The man, big and in a sort of black track suit, had come out from between the trees and was following along behind. He walked on, not taking any notice. Then he heard a shout, and turned round again. The man was much nearer and as he looked back at him, Max began to feel uneasy. He could see his face now and there was something about him that wasn't right. He was walking in a funny way for a start – sort of sideways, looking over his shoulder all the time, and he had an odd smile. Lots of shiny teeth. He waved at Max.

'Out for a walk? Lovely day, isn't it? Why don't we go along together? And you can talk to me.' He was smiling . . . and staring, in a peculiar way. For no reason, Max began to feel alarmed. He didn't smile back.

'You look a nice boy, don't run away . . . What's your name?'

He was quite close now, pale and overweight, with a reddish fuzz of hair and a tattoo snaking up one bare arm. 'What's your name?' he said again, still smiling in a kind of let's-pretend-we're-great-friends-sort-of-way. 'Got something in the van I think you'd like. I'll show you.'

'No thanks.' Head down, Max walked on quickly, his mouth dry and heart thumping uncomfortably.

Somewhere very near, a blackbird suddenly exploded into a clattering, scolding alarm, shattering the quiet, and for an instant the man turned his head away to look. Max started running – something he was good at. The second fastest runner in the school, he had been selected for the relay race in the county sports competition and had been training hard for weeks. Now he sped along the flinty forestry road faster than he had ever run in his life. He wasn't sure why, but he knew he had to get away, get to safety, home if possible. At first he heard some shouting and he thought there were footsteps behind him, but on no account was he stopping. When he got to the point where the track divided, one part leading off down towards the town, he could hardly breathe, but he kept on running. Then, as the track curved round to the right and he thought his feet were really not going to lift up and down any more, he saw an elderly couple ahead, dog on a lead. He rushed after them, breath coming in shallow gasps.

'You're in a hurry, young man,' the woman said.

'Nice day for running.' This was her husband. 'Where are you off to, then?'

'Home.' He looked back at the path, hardly able to speak. No black-clad figure there now, but he knew it couldn't be far away.

'Why are you wearing pyjamas?' the woman asked.

'Doing it for a bet,' he said when he had got his breath back a little. 'Sort of sponsored run and – er, walk thing. For my school.'

'In pyjamas? Which school is that?' asked the woman.

'Got to go,' mumbled Max, and started running again.

'Can we go to the zoo now?'

'*No*, Sammy!'

'Why? He hasn't come home –'

'Will you *shut up*, Sammy!' roared Donald.

They were in the kitchen going over it all again for the millionth time. Round and round in circles.

'He's an eldest child.' Eve stared at the mug of cold tea on the table before her.

'So what? You spoil him,' Donald said.

'As a youngest you wouldn't understand –'

'Explain it to me then. Why does he do these things?'

'He's – oh God, here's the policeman back'.

Police Officer Baines was young, freshly shaven, innocent-looking. What can he know about this sort of thing, Eve thought as they stood on the rough grass they called a lawn. He had talked to Sammy and admired his new bike for a moment, glanced round at the toys, footballs, trampoline with a wet picture-book that had been on it for days.

'Outhouses are all okay,' he said, 'and I've checked any wells on the farm. Filled in years ago, all mains now of course.' A pause. 'This is an old cottage, you haven't forgotten one somewhere? A well, I mean? Out in the garden? . . . No.' He wrote something down in his notebook. 'Has he got any friends in the village he might run off to?'

'Not in the village. Jack is his best friend,' Eve said. 'They –'

'That's four miles away!' Donald interrupted.

'Well, he might have got a lift? Tried to . . . ?' Eve's voice cracked and she didn't finish her sentence.

'They do sometimes get quite far,' the police officer said. 'On the other hand, some just hide – you know, nearby, and enjoy it all, the fuss. A bid for attention, you could say.'

'I'll go and phone Jack's parents,' Donald said. 'What's the number, Eve? Did you ever run off, worry your parents to death like this, officer?'

'I hid all day under the gooseberry bushes in my grand-mother's garden one time,' the young man said, smiling. 'Listened to them shouting, calling my name.'

'What happened when they found you?' Donald hesitated at the kitchen door, frowning.

'Not much. My dad wanted to wallop me, but my gran didn't let him. I think they docked my pocket money.'

'Good idea,' Donald said, disappearing into the kitchen.

During this conversation, Eve had been staring out towards the fields beyond the orchard, the beech hangars rising up to the blue sky. A perfect summer day, she thought, except it might turn out to be the worst day of my life. She hadn't known anything about children when she married, hadn't really wanted to know, wrapped up in her job as she was. And Max had suffered. Of course he has, she thought, tears starting to trickle down her cheeks again. I should have been more patient, tried to . . . She gave a sudden exclamation. Picked out by the bright sunlight, a small figure dressed in dark green was moving slowly across one of the fields beyond the orchard.

'There he is! Oh, God . . . *Donald!*'

'Daddy, daddy!' Sammy rushed away towards the door into the kitchen.

In the end, they let Police Officer Baines walk to the boundary fence to talk to Max. Eve was half-laughing, half in tears, Donald cautiously relieved but prepared to be the disciplinarian. They watched as the conversation took place and then Max walked across the grass towards them. He looked grave and very small, a long scratch down one side of his face.

'He didn't enjoy himself up there very much, apparently,' the young policeman said. 'Glad to be home. I think he's sorry he worried you. He knows it is a serious matter. Don't you, young man?' Max nodded speechlessly.

'Well, that's something, I suppose,' Donald said, still looking stern.

'Oh Max!' whispered Eve as she gathered him up and held him close to her. She kissed the top of his head 'We've been so worried! Don't ever do that again?'

'Not in your pyjamas, anyway,' Donald said gruffly.

They all laughed except Max, who stared at them blindly, ashen-faced. Crossing the field, it had come to him as clear as the bright sun in the sky, the long grass underfoot, that he was not the same person as the Max who had led his men up to the woods in the morning. Everything had changed. Now it was as if, lurking behind every tree, every path, every corner of his existence, something horrible had become visible – or half visible – that he hadn't known about before . . . Dangerous, shameful. Nothing was as it seemed and never had been. And he knew as a certainty, that he would not be seeing the faithful men of the Mountain Bike Unit again. They had left him, melted away, and would never be back. Tears filled his eyes and when Eve put her arms round him again, he sagged against her, choking and sobbing.

Elspeth's Garden

E lspeth stood looking out at the open expanse of sky above the high netted wall opposite, imagining the playing fields, school buildings beyond. She could hear children's voices and, every now and then, a whistle sounded shrilly. Below her, the narrow road, with its outrageous traffic-calming humps and patchwork of contrasting tarmac repairs, remained little used except for one or two cars, the odd cyclist taking a short cut.

She read through the letter again.

Dear Ms Wainright,
Re. Will of the late Mrs M.E.D. Dawson of Glenmore House, Bournemouth.

I write to tell you that you have been named in the will of your Great Aunt, Mrs Millicent Eliza Daisy Dawson deceased, as a beneficiary. Would you please be good enough to contact this office to make an appointment, as we need to take Instructions.

Yours truly,
W. Fennimore
Fennimore and Crouch Solicitors

She did have a vague memory of visiting an old lady with her mother at some time, but nothing about her or where she fitted in to the family. Had her brother Alistair received a similar letter, she wondered? And might there be some money? That would come in useful at the moment.

Standing by the open window, turning it over in her mind, she caught sight of solemn-faced Gary pushing his mother in her wheelchair along the pavement below. She waved at them, but he didn't look up. She thought how small he looked compared to the bulk of his mother: she was putting on weight. Last summer, he had stopped outside the gate with a heavy bag of shopping, so tired and hot under his shock of black hair that she had offered him a glass of water and then a second one. And from then on, if she was out in the front clipping something or watering her tomatoes, he sometimes stopped on his way back from school to sit on her front step and chat for a few minutes; watch what she was doing. He told her he liked tomatoes, would lke to grow some too, was saving for a camera and that he was nearly eleven. As soon as he had got the camera, he said, he would take a photo of her garden.

When she saw him in the street again a week or two later, she asked him how the saving was coming along.

'All the Saturday morning jobs round here have gone,' he said, looking dejected.

'Oh! Well why don't you come and do some weeding for me, then, that's a job – paid, I mean? And you would be doing me a favour, the brick patio at the back always needs weeding.'

Since then, he often turned up on a Saturday morning. He seemed quite chatty and was much more cheerful. She looked forward to his visits.

'We've got to describe our favourite animal for our biology project at school,' he said, walking in to the kitchen one Saturday morning. 'Drawings and photographs and everything we can find out. I've borrowed Dad's old mobile ... I'm doing foxes!'

'What made you choose them?' she asked.

'There was a programme on TV about a man who bred tame foxes.'

'I am not sure you can ever tame a fox,' she said.

'My friend Donald found a cub – quite small, grey fur – round the back of the flats. So I took it home –'

'What happened?'

'Mum couldn't stand the smell, so Dad put it out on the balcony. But it wasn't there in the morning so it must have chewed through the box – it was only cardboard – and fallen off in the night.'

'Oh dear,' she said, thinking how matter-of-fact he sounded. 'Well, I often see them around here. Just come in to the garden through the side door and have a look when you want.'

When she had first started at the garden centre and was only renting one floor from Mr Binner – still living at Primrose Villas after the death of his wife – she had known there were foxes in the wilderness down at the end of the garden; occasionally caught sight of one slipping through the dense green vegetation, or trotting along one of the crumbling boundary walls. And in winter, then as now, she often heard the ghastly strangled scream of the vixen. Sometimes, she wondered if one of them might sneak up and grab her cat Fisher, still almost a kitten and too friendly for his own good. A few weeks ago, she had seen a big dog fox curled up asleep in the long grass of what she called her 'lawn'.

'Vermin,' Alistair said briefly when she told him. 'They stink and crap everywhere. You should get the pest control people in.'

'Foxes are not actually vermin,' she said. 'And they eat rats!' She knew this from Gary, who had turned out to be a mine of information about wild life in general and foxes in particular.

'Since when have you been such an expert?' Alistair asked. 'Foxes get mange . . . spread disease.' He wrinkled his nose. 'By the way, that cat litter tray in the downstairs toilet is disgusting. Unhygienic.'

'Fisher is still just a kitten,' she said. 'He's not used to other cats yet. He'll be going out in the garden soon.'

'That's unhygienic too,' Alistair said. 'Where did you hang my coat?'

Alistair had always been exceptionally fastidious about dirt, germs, things out of kilter in any way. Fruit was especially suspect, and had to be washed several times and preferably peeled before he would touch it; books had to be in book shelves and arranged in alphabetical order; clothes – his own and other people's – must be clean, in drawers or cupboards and hung up on the right hanger. Personal hygiene was a huge issue and always had been. He washed his hands for at least ten minutes after visiting the bathroom and was always complaining that her house was 'filthy'. She was not clear exactly why, but she thought this might be the result of losing his mother so young? Although she had been young too, thrust into the role of little mother at only ten. Her father had to work hard and was often away, so he relied on a succession of foreign girls – what else could he do? Some of them were nice, or even very nice, but others were not. She remembered a sallow-faced Parisian who had made five-year-old Alistair sit at the table until four o'clock because he wouldn't eat his spinach. Poor Alistair she thought. No wonder he is like he is.

She had found Fennimore and Crouch on Google easily enough – a city firm of obvious respectability – and wondered again whether Alistair knew about the bequest? He had been very much against her buying Number 3.

'Buy a place in *this* neighbourhood?' was his comment when she mentioned that her landlord had offered to sell her the cottage. 'I'm surprised you haven't been mugged yet. Why not move upmarket into a decent neighbourhood?'

'I have lived here for nearly twenty-five years and not been mugged,' she said. 'Anyway, I can't afford "upmarket". *I* don't get paid a million pound bonus like –'

'It's not a million. Be realistic, Elspeth. At your age, you need a nice modern flat on a ground floor, cheaper to maintain –'

'But I like it here!'

'You can't! I mean, those hideous council blocks at the end of the road! What sort of people live in them?'

'Just ordinary people.'

'All on benefit, I wouldn't wonder.' She let this pass.

'Well, it's quiet and I love the garden.'

'I don't know why,' he said – she let that pass as well. 'And another thing,' he began, leaning forward to look out at the garden. 'Oh! There's someone out there – a boy, a black boy!' Alistair sounded disapproving. 'Who is he? Needs a haircut!'

'Yes. Gary,' she said. 'He sometimes comes in on Saturday

mornings to help me in the garden. I think his father is from Uganda.'

'Where does he live?'

'In one of those blocks at the end of the street.'

'Do you know anything about him?'

'What sort of thing? They live on the eleventh floor.'

'Well, is he alright? Honest, I mean?'

'Why shouldn't he be? His mother is in a wheelchair and his dad works at the printers in Glossop Street. Alistair, I am going down to the kitchen to make coffee –'

What *is* the matter with him she thought, wrenching open the kitchen drawer with a clatter. He is getting worse!

'You should get a proper coffee machine,' Alistair said, watching as she poured boiling water into the cafetière. 'I've just bought a new one. It makes marvellous coffee.'

As he stood there Fisher, who had been rubbing his furry body against her legs, purring, jumped up on to the table.

'Can't you get your cat not to do that?' Alistair said. 'Cats can transmit all kinds of serious infections, you know.'

She felt relieved but also deflated when he had gone, suddenly consumed by anxiety. Perhaps he's right, she thought. It *is* a bleak area. The surviving small cottages and villas in her narrow 'cut-through' were very much a minority among the tower blocks. And the huge trafficked road grinding towards the City, with its reputation for drug dealing and crime, was only a couple of streets away – she could hear it now, rumbling faintly. Suppose I am making a mistake? As for the garden, she sighed. Facing south, the front aspect was lovely: cucumbers and pots of geraniums, tomato plants on the front steps basking in the sun, but then there was the rest of it. In the far distant past, either it had all been one large unbroken piece of land, or the neighbouring rear gardens had at some time been amalgamated with hers, the other properties being left with mere strips in comparison. Her garden was enormous – and out of control, she thought.

The Binner parents had fled to Britain as refugees, taking their only son and leaving a thriving antique business behind. Not long after arriving in Britain, the father got ill and then died – from grief, Mr Binner told her later. After the war, and as the nearest surviving relative, he had received sizable reparations, and started buying up property with the money: large houses and their gardens that were going cheap in un-fashionable areas of London at that time. Later on, and as a contrast perhaps, he had bought Primrose Villas, a row of little Regency cottages; kept one for himself and his wife, and sold the others – acquired the neighbouring gardens, perhaps? Mrs Binner had been very particular, it seemed, and they had employed a man full-time to cut the grass, prune the roses and look after the apple and pear trees. But then his wife died and he had lost interest, retired from property and rented out most of the rooms. One of his first tenants was Elspeth who, in due course, graduated to the ground floor and two rooms in the basement, while her landlord continued to live upstairs..

Mr Binner had a soft spot for Elspeth. 'Your kind face cheers me up,' he would say. 'Why haven't you got a nice husband?'

'I did,' she said, 'but he went off with someone!'

'Then he was a fool,' Mr Binner said. 'You were well rid of him.'

In Berlin, his parents had been well-known collectors

and dealers, and he had continued the family tradition in a
small way, antique silver being his speciality. Occasionally he
showed her some modest item on which he expected to make
a good price: a very small but exquisite cherry-wood box
with a silver lid, and a swan's-down powder puff inside; interesting bits of china; a tiny ivory frame containing a miniature
painting of a coach and three spirited horses dashing across
snow, the coachman cracking a whip over their flying manes.
It could be dated to the time before the last Czar of Russia was
murdered, he told her. When finally, well into his eighties,
he had retreated to comfortable sheltered housing in Golders
Green, he suggested that she rent the cottage for a relatively
modest sum and look after it for him. She agreed at once.
Now, he had offered to sell it to her. Raising the mortgage
money had been, and still was, a major issue, the truth being
that she couldn't really afford it. Perhaps Great Aunt Daisy's
bequest might help or even solve the problem, she thought.

Over time, she had imposed some sort of order near the house
at the back. A brick patio with some rickety chairs and a table,
a square of grass Gary cut with a pair of rusty shears now and
then; a tub of spearmint and lavender. The mint had escaped
from the tub and was now growing outwards through the
bricks. Beyond the bricks, a sort of no-man's-land of weed and
bramble blanketed the receding ground, ivy slowly throttling
Mathilde Binner's shrubs and fruit trees grown to giant pro-
portions or fallen into the grass. In summer, a surviving rose
or two lifted its head above the nettles and long grass, and the
smell of wild garlic was everywhere. Just inside the vestigial
boundary wall at the far end and hardly visible, the remains of

some sort of small building crouched under its burden of ivy. Large trees in the rear gardens of the street that backed onto hers added to the impression that she was living on the edge of a forest.

Alistair – who travelled extensively on behalf of the government in some exotic financial capacity or other, she could never quite grasp what he actually did – had two properties himself: a flat in the Barbican and an immaculate and beautiful house just outside Rome. She had stayed with him there several times, and on each occasion was completely stunned by the beauty of the place.

'How can you bear to leave it?' she had asked once.

'Oh! I'd die of boredom after two minutes if I stayed too long,' he said. 'Perhaps I'll retire here? Not that I am planning to retire,' he added quickly.

She sometimes wondered about Alistair. Secretaries retrieved his gloves, scarf, papers, whatever he had misled most recently, chivvied him to his meetings; and there had been girlfriends, even a wife for a short period. But recently she had been seeing much more of him, and guessed he might be lonely. He certainly talked a lot, mostly about himself or the various offices or institutions he had to do with, never about the people in them. She no longer thought it odd. Number 3, Primrose Villas was on his route to and from the airport; so, increasingly often, he would get out of the taxi and call in on her, rather than go home.

Today, he was returning from some important government business in Geneva and had stopped in before taking the cab on to the Barbican. He had gone on and on about the rear garden.

'If you are going to buy this place, Else, you really must do something about all *that*,' he said, staring out of the window. 'Get the pest control people in.'

'You mean get rid of the wildlife? I.e., foxes?'

'Sell it,' Alistair interrupted. 'Get planning permission to build something there.'

'Alistair, it's not mine . . . and the mortgage isn't settled yet.'

'Aren't you a bit old for mortgages?'

'I have some savings, but with a mortgage . . .' She took a deep breath and mentioned the amount she was trying to raise.

'Well, that won't buy a chicken coop,' Alistair said.

Mr Fennimore proved to be exactly as she had imagined: a small neat man of indeterminate age, speaking to her from the other side of a very large desk about the last will and testament of Millicent Eliza Daisy Dawson.

'Mrs Dawson had reached the age of one hundred and four when she passed away. A strong constitution. She was a client of this firm for eighty-seven years,' he said as she sat down.

'Did my aunt know that I have a brother?'

'I do not recall any discussion on the matter,' Mr Fennimore said. 'But your aunt was not a lady much given to discussion.' He adjusted his glasses carefully. 'First there is the cheque – in the sum of a thousand pounds – which will be paid into your bank. Please be sure you give us the address and account number you wish it to be paid into . . .' She stopped listening. A *thousand pounds*? She felt as if someone had suddenly slammed a door in her face. It's watching too many happy endings on TV, she thought. I'll have to raise more money for the mortgage somehow . . . Could I steel myself to ask Alistair?

The solicitor's voice broke in to her jumble of thoughts.

'Miss Wainwright? Ah – do you have a broker who will deal with the investments?'

'I expect my brother will know what to do with those.'

He glanced at the document in his hand again.

'Now we come to the chattels, items that she directed should be given to you, as well as the legacy and list of investments. The remainder of the contents will be disposed of as the will directs.'

'What about my brother?'

'You are the sole beneficiary, Miss Wainwright.'

He showed her photographs of the furniture – heavy and dark, and of a size that would be impossible to fit into any normal living room. This was to be sold to raise money for charity. The same for the clothes – apart from the mink coat, which was to be given to the chauffeur.

'Mrs Dawson employed a lady driver in her latter years,' Mr Fennimore murmured. 'The remaining chattels are to be given to you, Miss Wainwright. A large quantity of monogrammed Irish linen, some silver – which I advise you to have valued – and there is a train set belonging to Mrs Dawson's deceased nephew, Flight Lieutenant William Dawson.'

Elspeth took the bus home feeling distinctly gloomy. Of course, it was kind of the mythical Great Aunt Daisy to think of her, but a thousand pounds was neither here nor there, and what on earth was she to do with the Irish linen, or the train set for that matter? Perhaps she could sell them? She sighed. I can't bear to ask Alistair for money she thought. I'll just have to try and borrow some more from the bank – or go back to the garden centre part time.

★

Negotiations over Number 3 seemed interminable. She understood that the two sets of solicitors had to go through preliminary enquiries, but it had been months. Periodically the solicitor assured her that these things were always slow; there had been a delay regarding the deeds and the Land Registry, but now everything was progressing well. Meantime he sent her a large bill. Then one afternoon he telephoned to say that a slight problem had arisen. Was she aware of the existence of a right of way over the property? The mortgage company had been in touch and wanted to know who owned it.

'Right of way?'

'From the street at the front of the property to some sort of – is there a building in the back garden?'

'No – well, only a sort of fallen-down brick thing covered in ivy. At the rear.'

'I see. Who is the owner?'

'Mr Binner, I suppose?'

'The vendor? We will make enquiries.'

They will have a hard job making any enquiries of Mr Binner, she thought. He doesn't remember anything much these days – apart from his rheumatism and the state of his bowels, poor man.

Her inherited silver turned out to be about twenty-five blackened spoons, several pairs of candlesticks, and a number of bulky heavily-embossed objects, presumably silver, whose function remained mysterious, all of it wrapped in layers of newspaper. Just right for the next jumble sale, she thought, but I'll show it to Mr Binner first, just in case. He may not remember which day it is but he will know about the silver. Now for the train set.

She had removed some of the newspaper wrapping and was holding up a black locomotive and tender when Gary knocked on the side door, looking extremely cheerful.

'It's half term,' he announced. 'There's definitely a den under that pile of bricks near the boundary wall, and I've photographed the vixen drinking out of your birdbath.'

'That's great, Gary!'

'And I borrowed Dad's smartphone,' he said. 'His friend at work is going to help me get the photos ready for printing at the weekend when, when –' He glanced at the floor. 'Is that a train set?'

'Looks like it. Yes.'

The train tracks were tied together in bundles. Some had three lines, some two, and there seemed to be a lot of them. There were two locomotives and four cream-and-brown Pullman carriages, each of which had little pink shaded lights in the windows. The newspaper wrappings were all dated September 1939 – which must be when Flight Lieutenant Dawson's mother had packed it all away, she thought.

'Who does it belong to?'

'Me,' she said after a moment.

'Does it work?' Gary held up a bundle of rails. 'These are all different sizes.'

'I don't know. The engine looks almost new. I'll ask Alistair. He had a model railway when he was young.'

They left the circle of rails and the locomotive with its tender and carriages set up beneath the kitchen table, and Gary picked up his bags: the lift at the flats had broken down again and his mother was stuck. After he had gone, she smoothed out the newspaper and began to read about Britain on the verge of the war that was going to kill Flight Lieutenant William Dawson. She was still leaning on the table, reading, when the solicitor rang.

'I need to consult you,' he began. 'Nothing serious, but it seems that the easement that has been granted – '

'The what?'

'The easement, right of way ... Mentioning the prospective buyer and his or her heir and assigns is proving difficult – '

'Where does the right of way go? It must lead somewhere?'

'You mentioned that there is another building on your land?'

'There was. Derelict now. A few bricks covered in ivy.'

'That will be it. Mentioned in the original deeds as a small stable, accessed via the common land at the southern end of your property. In 1880 the then owner – an organist at St Stephen's, now demolished – gave an easement to the church reverend in order that he might take his pony – which pulled the trap – to a small stable on the boundary of your property. A new arrangement was required as the adjoining common land, from which access had been obtained previously, was being developed. So access to a number of stables along the boundary disappeared, including that of the reverend.'

'But it's all so long ago,' she said.

'Not as far as the law is concerned, Miss Wainwright. Unfortunately there is no record of the right of way being rescinded, even though, by the sound of it, currently the stable is no longer in a viable condition. But the mortgage company – '

'Have you asked Mr Binner?'

'The vendor claims to know nothing about it. Failing to use an easement is not in itself sufficient ... but the owner must make it clear, that he or she ...' He was speaking slowly and carefully, as if he were trying to convince himself that what he was saying was what he meant. 'And abandonment will not be inferred . . . the principle being that a person cannot have rights against himself.'

What was he talking about? She had lost the thread.

'Shall I mention it to the vendor? I've known him a long time.'

'You can try.'

'I'll telephone him.'

Mr Binner looked older and considerably more fragile, although still full of his wispy absent-minded charm. Really, he might blow away in a strong wind, she thought.

'So nice to be asked to tea.' He clasped her arm with trembling fingers. 'You probably heard I have not been too well? Troubles in the "unmentionable" department.'

'Oh dear, poor you,' she said. She had heard about the unmentionable department ever since she first met Mr Binner.

'But I have brought something to show you.' He searched in his pockets. 'Ah!' He held out a small silver object for Elspeth to inspect. 'A snuff box belonging to George the First.'

'How do you know it belonged to him?'

'Got his name on it!' he said, smiling at her.

'Mr Binner . . .' She pulled herself together. 'I asked you to tea because something has cropped up which affects me buying Number Three. A right of way across the garden has been discovered, and I have to find the owner. Do you understand?'

'Right of way?' he echoed vaguely. He was gazing across the kitchen at the dresser as if in a sort of trance. 'What are those spoons?'

'I inherited them. There are those too.' She pointed at the collection of candlesticks and other blackened objects on the bottom shelf of the dresser.

'Where did you say they – ?'

'My great aunt.'

'The spoons look like William and Mary, solid sterling silver . . . About 1730,' he said, clearly captivated. 'Where did you find them?'

'I inherited them,' she said again. 'Mr Binner, I need to know about this right-of-way thing. Who owns it at present?' But he wasn't listening.

'Did you realise how valuable they are?'

'No, I didn't. But until I know who, if anyone, still owns the right of way over your garden, I am going to have trouble with the mortgage. And if I can't get a mortgage' – she raised her voice – 'I can't buy Number Three!'

He looked at her, startled.

'Right of way? That's all been settled, I think.'

'But that's the point!' She gritted her teeth. 'It hasn't been settled.'

'I do recall someone speaking to me about something similar recently. Perhaps I should ask my stepson.'

'I didn't know you had a stepson.'

'Lives in LA,' Mr Binner said, picking up one of the spoons. 'I would estimate that this spoon is worth at least seventeen thousand! More, probably. How many are there?'

'We could always go elsewhere for a mortgage of course,' the solicitor said the following morning. 'With the proviso that you accept the consequences of a possible owner of the right turning up. Apply to formally remove the right? But any successors in title would have to agree, and you would have to prove that the land has fallen out of use. For the right of way to be properly extinguished, then both the dominant land – the land with the right to an easement or profit – and the servient land –'

'Servient?'

'It will be for you to prove that the right has fallen into disuse, that the requisite amount of time has passed –'

'But I've lived here for nearly twenty-five years and nobody has mentioned it or walked along it, and the so-called stable has been a ruin since before I moved in.'

'I am aware of that, but as it's a deeded right it may be a case of entering a Deed of Release, Miss Wainwright. Which means time,' he added. And money, she thought.

In the kitchen ten minutes later, waiting for the kettle to boil, she was brooding over Mr Binner's remarks about the spoons (she must not start fantasising about them as well) when Gary tapped at the side door. He was jubilant.

'Look!' he said handing her a large packet. 'Mum said to show you. I've got to choose two for my project . . . by Monday. Not too big.'

One by one she studied the photographs in detail, impressed at how clear and convincing the images were: the thin little vixen gazing straight out from the freckled gloom under the big elms at the bottom of the garden, the cubs chasing and scuffling through patches of bramble.

'Gary, I'm impressed! How on earth did you get so many? Are they really all taken on a mobile?'

'Yep. Dad's smartphone, and his friend at the printers did the enlarging and printed them out. Here's a bigger one of the vixen in the dustbin area near the flats. I tied a bone to one of the down pipes one evening and just waited. It's not very clear because it's evening time. I have to choose two. Which is your favourite?'

'All of them,' she said.

On the following Saturday she had taken her morning cup of tea into the garden in her dressing gown when Gary turned up unusually early.

'My project got a special mention!' he said at once. 'And the school is going to send me and another boy on a special visit to a zoo out in the country to talk to the keepers there and see the work in the small mammals department.'

'Gary! How exciting! I'm so pleased.'

He held up a flat parcel wrapped in brown paper and thrust it at her. 'This photo of the vixen is for you,' he said, his face shining with pleasure and pride. He looked so animated and happy she felt like picking him up and whirling him round the room.

'Thank you! Can I take it downstairs?' She was laughing. 'I haven't had my breakfast yet.'

The kitchen seemed dark after the sunshine. She turned on the light to see the photograph better and Gary caught sight of the circle of railway tracks under the table where they had left them. He picked up the black locomotive and fitted it onto the track.

'How does this work? Is it electric?'

'I'm not sure.' They were still on their knees, gazing at the track, when they heard the door bell and some knocking upstairs.

'I suppose it *is* quite an old model,' she said, getting to her feet. 'Just a minute, must be the postman.'

Standing in the hall, Alistair had been apologetic (for him). He had texted her but obviously she hadn't received it? He had arrived on an early-morning flight, and thought he might pop in for breakfast on the way home.

'Is that alright?' he asked, rather uncharacteristically

'Fine. Come downstairs,' she said, 'I was just going to have breakfast.'

In the kitchen, stretched out full-length on the floor, Gary was pushing the black locomotive and its tender round the two loops of railway track, the brown carriages hitched on behind.

'Hi!' he said, eyes fixed resolutely on what he was doing.

'Good heavens! What have you got there? That's a Basset-Locke steam engine and tender! Hornby Doublo!' Alistair's face changed – as if he were witnessing a miraculous vision of some kind, she thought. '*And* you have an electric locomotive and tender there too! Where on earth have they come from?' He clapped his hands like a delighted child.

'Great Aunt Daisy,' Elspeth said. 'Her nephew's train set.'

'But they are museum pieces!'

'Do they work?' Gary looked up at him.

Alistair threw his coat onto a chair, and Elspeth watched as he got down on his knees.

'The engine with the green trim is electric. This one' – he took the black engine and its tender from Gary – 'is fuelled by methylated spirits. There's a long sliding metal container under the boiler – somewhere here?' He bent down so that his nose was inches from the floor. 'Fill that with meths, slide it back into place, light it, and off you go! A proper steam engine! You have to make sure there's water in the boiler, of course.' He sat back on his heels. 'I had one of them when I was about your age.'

'What about this?' Gary picked up one of the cream-and-tan carriages.

'Either engine will pull those,' Alistair said. 'But if they are on the three-railed electric tracks, the windows in the carriages should light up. Is there a transformer? Yes, there it is . . . We could try! Got any meths in the house, Else?' Alistair asked, beaming – Elspeth couldn't remember seeing him so animated for years. He looks happy, she thought, smiling. They both do.

'It's in such good condition!' Alistair said. 'What's your name again, young man?'

'Gary.'

'Of course,' Alistair said.

She found a bottle with half an inch of meths still showing and left them on the kitchen floor, completely absorbed; took her tea and toast upstairs and into the garden to sit in the only deckchair. It was very warm, a couple of doves sidling about on the roof murmuring gently, and she had begun to relax, forget about everything, when Gary appeared suddenly.

'Someone to see you,' he said. 'Some old guy . . .'

Mr Binner stood in the hall looking both fragile and determined.

'Have you had it valued?' he asked at once.

'You mean the silver? I only saw you a couple of days ago.'

'You must be very careful what cleaning agents you use.'

'Mr Binner!' She had been going to say, 'I don't have either time or the inclination to spend polishing up old silver spoons,' but he interrupted her.

'I would offer to help, my dear, but it ought to be done professionally. And there's the insurance. I could give you an approximate valuation, if you like?' She could see that he was determined to give her one, whether she wanted it or not.

When Mr Binner mentioned the valuation figures he had in mind, she laughed and stared disbelievingly at him. Perched on the edge of his chair, he had taken each piece out of the box and told her what he thought it was worth. Even halved and allowing for the customary exaggeration, it added up to a staggering amount, way over any figure she had imagined. Now that he had taken a taxi home − after extracting the promise that she would contact her insurance broker *today* − she was left gazing at the pile of blackened objects on her sitting-room floor. Mr Binner had been retired for many years and was in fact now very old. Could he really still be in touch with the current antique silver world? The market could have changed without him noticing. Her doubts grew; it was all much too good to be true. There was always some sort of snag, in her experience, and it would be the same here. Look at that ridiculous right-of-way thing popping up at the last moment. Who could have predicted that? She wondered if her solicitor had talked to the Los Angeles stepson? Perhaps there was some news? She was reaching for her mobile when she heard Alistair shouting up the stairs.

'Elspeth? Are you there? The taxi man's back! Wants to see you!'

'Me? Why? What's happened? Is it Mr Binner?'

'Nothing to worry about,' the red-faced cabbie reassured her. 'The old gentleman said he meant to give you this document here.' He handed her a large oblong envelope. 'It slipped his mind, he said, but it was very important that you have it and I must get it to you at once. Personal, like. The fare is all paid up,' he added.

Sitting down at the table with Fisher on her knee, she began to read. There were approximately six or seven densely printed pages of text, entitled 'Deed of Release March 1987, 3 Primrose Villas, London'. Despite the antiquated, largely incomprehensible legal language, the various headings concerning 'Easement over Parcel of Land' and the like suggested what it was about: that idiotic right of way! The document had been signed by Leon Berthold Binner and Esther Mathilde Binner, and witnessed. A map, also signed, showed a 'parcel of land' marked in red which clearly corresponded with the boundaries of her existing garden. No doubt about that, there it was! Folded away with all this, she found a separate sheet of stiff foolscap on which she recognised Mr Binner's trembling hand.

My dear Child,

I mentioned the problem to Carl, my stepson. And he reminded me that he had sorted out the so called 'Right of Way' problem in 1987. Therefore he said I should forward the enclosed documents to you, which I now have much pleasure in doing.

Affectionately yours,

Berthold Binner

Somehow, she thought, Mr B had managed to locate the relevant documents and stuffed them into his pocket, intending to give them to her. But diverted by the silver, had omitted to do so. However, discovering the envelope still in his pocket on arriving back at Golders Green, he had paid the taxi driver to make a return journey and deliver it for him. Which must mean he believes it is important, she thought with a stab of excitement. Mr Binner was not the sort of man to spend money on taxis without a good reason.

Oblivious to Flight Lieutenant Dawson's Basset-Locke locomotive and tender trundling round at her feet, she began to read through every line of the document again, studying the map in detail. Second time round the archaic language did not seem so obscure, and the map made everything very plain. Stroking Fisher's soft fur, she reached the concluding page for a second time, relief and optimism flooding through her. It's all quite clear if you read it carefully, she thought.

'Else, have you noticed that the pink lights in the Pullman carriages actually light up?' asked Alistair from the floor. 'Barry here got the transformer going. Wonderful, isn't it?'

'Yes, wonderful,' she said, looking at his relaxed happy face and Gary's delight as he watched the twinkling little lights bustling round under the table. 'A kind of miracle, I would say.'

The Mill Pond

F raser had just finished a quick lunch at his club when one of the other members came over to him.

'Fraser! Have a look at this!' He held up a copy of *The Times*. 'Unique salt-water mill in the West Country – isn't this your old place?' Fraser's description of his childhood home had obviously stuck in his mind. 'It's for sale!'

'For sale?' echoed Fraser. 'Let me see.' He read through the advertisement. Within hours, he had telephoned the estate agent and arranged to drive down with his sister to look at Mill View, as it was now called.

Fraser was not an imaginative man – indeed, many people might have said that his powers of imagination were almost nil – but throughout his life the image of this huddle of buildings on the edge of a muddy creek had become a kind of vision of something essential that he had lost, hallucinatory in its power. He gazed around him at the garden, lichen-covered apple trees, low grey slated house and barn, four-acre mill pond gleaming beyond the pale bleached slates of the roof; listened to the familiar sound of seabirds squabbling in the mud; and was almost overcome by emotion. How old was he when his family were forced out? Eight? Ten?

'But James, this is derelict!' his sister said as they walked through the length of the house together. 'How long has it been empty?' She had been a baby when they had left and re-membered nothing.

'I don't know . . . Some years.'

'There are ferns growing out of the bedroom wall.'

'Yes . . .'

'It's going to cost millions.'

'Probably,' Fraser said, looking out of the kitchen window at the sheet of water stretching away towards the further side of the creek.

'But what will you *do* here? Do you know anyone?'

'I don't particularly *want* to know anyone, thanks.'

'Well, it's not exactly overcrowded,' she said.

'There's more land down the road,' Fraser murmured after a few minutes. 'And a couple of garages – part of the package.'

Bigger than a cottage and smaller than a house, Mill View stood at a slightly higher level than the garage, the front win-dows looking out over the millpond. The lane ended below in a rough stony sweep where a few blades of thin grass struggled to survive, and a miniature quay. Behind, a small cramped cottage with a porch faced out towards the mill pond.

'Is the cottage yours too?'

'No, I plan to buy it though – and the garage.'

'Who is the owner?'

'No idea.'

He waved at the two big doors separating the cottage from the larger Mill View.

'Two garages there now . . . Used to be a hay loft and space for carts.'

They walked onto the quay. It was high tide and the mill pond stretched away from them in a smooth, quiet expanse of water gleaming in the afternoon light. Grey mullet swirled just beneath the surface, occasionally flipping up to leave diminishing concentric rings behind.

'I always wanted a boat as a lad,' he said. 'I –'

He broke off, as behind them there was a sudden clatter and commotion. A woman had emerged from the cottage holding an enamel basin, and was now walking towards them, shouting.

'This is *private!*' She wagged her finger at them. 'All private down here.'

She was tall, bony, ravaged somehow, her face scowling and angry. Fraser, who had spent his life negotiating business deals with crooks of one sort and another, had a well-developed sense of who other people were. He knew at once that Mary Olson was the sort of human being who made trouble in the world if she could, indeed enjoyed making trouble.

'You can't park here!' she said again, flapping her arms as she spoke, voice loud and raucous. 'Visitors don't realise – it's all private. No parking!' She was swaying slightly. 'I try and keep it nice,' she continued angrily, 'but people just drive over my grass!' She pointed to the rear of his large, well-polished, very expensive vehicle.

'We are not staying long,' he said. (Which grass did she mean? The groundsel and thin blades poking up through the stony ground he was standing on?) 'We were just looking at next door. It's for sale?'

'That's right,' she said bitterly. 'Rich people, they come down here and splash their money around, think they own the place.' She glared at him. 'Strangers!'

Fraser contemplated the swaying figure. She's drunk, he thought, and held out his hand.

'James Fraser,' he said, 'and this is my sister Gill.'

'Mary,' she said after a pause. 'Pleased to meet you. On holiday, are you? Well, leave your car for a few minutes this time, then.'

She walked to the edge of the little quay and began to scatter potato peelings and other scraps into the water from the basin.

'Come on! Come on!' The harsh voice carried across the still water. 'My babies!' she said over her shoulder, tossing out the rest of the peelings. 'They don't like nobody else feeding them.' The two swans on the further side of the pond had started to paddle towards them. 'On holiday, are you?' she asked again, voice suddenly wheedling and confidential, over-friendly. She wiped her hands on the legs of her trousers. 'That's a nice car you've got there. I'll make a cup of tea if you like, show you round.'

'Thank you, but we'll be leaving soon,' Fraser said.

She swayed towards him, smiling, stained yellow dentures rather spoiling the effect.

'Be my guest,' she said.

In the car, driving back up the lane, Gill burst out laughing.

'What did that mean, for heaven's sake?'

'She was drunk,' Fraser said.

In the village they stopped for a beer and a sandwich, and Gill asked the publican about the woman they had encountered.

'Oh, Mary!' he said. 'Down at the mill? She's a right one, she is! Deaf as a drowned monkey and two-thirds crazy —'

'She likes the booze, Mary Olson does,' interrupted one of the regulars. 'And the men,' said another.

'Mr Olson was OK,' the publican said. 'Kept her in order. But he's been gone ten years or more. Wore out with old Mary at him night and day!' Everyone laughed. 'It was the nights, I reckon,' someone said to more laughter.

'I hope that woman isn't your only neighbour?' Gill said as they got back into the car.

'I'll have Bim with me,' Fraser said.

'Oh yes, I always forget about Bim,' Gill said.

The truth was that everyone forgot about Bim, including Fraser. Secretary, companion and lover, Bim had been rescued by Fraser from a destitute Thai family when he was a child and adopted. Unkind people said that the boy had been sold to him by desperate parents with too many children, but he seemed happy enough. At first he lived with Fraser in the big house on the edge of the park and went to a posh school nearby, where he did well; then, as an adolescent, watched as day by day Fraser's business expanded. A young man of few words and an excellent secretary, he ran Fraser's life with enviable calm and efficiency. Fraser would often say that he could not manage without Bim; and indeed, he seemed fond of him – in the way some people are fond of a dog or cat.

When Bim was told about Mill View, he listened politely but did not show any great enthusiasm: all that water and mud mystified him, he preferred the sun and the Italian lakes, or the villa on Capri, himself. But he knew about Fraser's unaccountable passion for the place and dutifully set about the process of acquiring it. In due course and after much negotiation the survey was completed – the price much reduced as a consequence – and ownership of Mill View passed into

Fraser's hands. A year later, when all the alterations and building work were finished, architects and garden designers paid off, he began to fly down for the odd weekend. Occasionally Bim accompanied him, but he preferred London.

When he first returned, despite his intention to secure her cottage in due course, Fraser neither saw nor thought much about the woman next door. He had made up his mind to buy the big field at the back first and, as Bim was a little out of his depth in this very rural environment, he began the complex negotiations with the local farmer himself. Once or twice he had caught sight of her while driving up the lane, or heard her cursing and shouting in her little yard at the side, but he took care to look the other way.

Come the spring, however, the field was his, and he began to relax. The whole place was fragrant with the scent of wild narcissi and daffodils, and when he was in residence he sometimes wandered out into the garden with a drink in the evening, surprised suddenly by the quiet beauty of the place.

Access to the main garden from the house was via a narrow grassy path which ran for a good few yards very close to his neighbour's yard and back garden – the only weak spot in the armour, as Fraser thought of it. Here, to his annoyance, he sometimes found himself ambushed by Next Door and forced to engage in an unwilling one-sided conversation. He tried ignoring her, but she followed along beside him on her side of the boundary, shouting remarks. Exasperated, he told Bim to get a hedge planted as soon as possible.

By the time of his next visit, a lorry-load of tall conifers in pots had been delivered which, when planted two deep and close together along the entire length of the boundary, made a dense high hedge taller than Fraser himself. It was an improvement – he did not have to see her – but often, if he was anywhere near, he would hear her: a shouted rambling monologue on the other side of the hedge. One day he stopped to listen.

'High and mighty bugger . . . Mr bloody Fraser this, bloody Fraser that! Thinks he owns the place . . . All that money. And his chink fancy boy . . . Needs taking down a peg, he does . . . Down a bloody peg.' She walked away, out of earshot.

On his side of the hedge Fraser found himself momentarily hot with anger. But managed to mutter, 'Leave it, don't get involved. She's round the bend.' All he had to do was use another door to access his garden. Occasionally, however, he found himself drawn towards the boundary hedge, impelled to listen. One day he shouted back:

'Why the fuck don't you shut up?'

'She can't hear you,' Bim said. 'She never will.'

In London, it was usually Bim who dealt with the car. At Mill View, however, occasionally Fraser got the car out from the garage himself. 'Slumming,' his sister said, laughing.

One morning – it must be at least two months since they were last at Mill View – Fraser had been 'caught' by his garage door. Already smelling strongly of alcohol, Mary was in a friendly ingratiating mood.

'Hello stranger! Come in and have a drink!' she said, smiling coquettishly through the car window. 'I want to talk to you!'

'Good morning,' he said. 'What about?'

'The grass.'

'Grass?'

'In the front.'

Memories of past negotiations with a motley array of crooks nudged at him. This could be his opportunity, perhaps. Surely if he could outwit a man like Cas Steinberg, legendary speculator on New York's stock exchange, he could tame a barmy, poverty-stricken, drunken old woman like Mary Olsen?

'What about a cup of tea this afternoon?' he said affably.

As soon as he was through the porch door, he knew it was a mistake. Mary had put her best foot forward – was that a wig? Bright red nail varnish shone at the end of her dirty old mis-shapen fingers; she had made up her face and put on a low-cut flimsy see-through sort of top. She looked like a raddled old tart out prospecting for clients. Eventually he accepted a half glass of appalling sweet sherry and sat, listening to her stream of invective which very quickly got round to the non-existent grass opposite his garage. How it was 'her land' and how 'people' drove their cars everywhere, nobody respected her and she would have to *do* something! Fraser nodded and smiled, made placatory comments, but it was obvious she couldn't or wouldn't hear him. Merely waved her glass in his face and repeated everything she had said before but louder. He sat there as long as he could stand it, but suddenly he had had enough. What was he doing, sitting here being harangued by a foul-mouthed wretched old hag? Abruptly he stood up, made some excuse about an expected phone call, and left.

'I'm going to have to get her out of that place,' he said to Bim. 'Pronto'.

They left Mill View that evening.

★

It was several months before they were at the cottage again, and this time Fraser decided he would like to play a round or two of golf while he was there. It was a good course and the clubhouse served excellent lunches; added to which, he had a longstanding invitation to join a colleague who, by chance, owned a bungalow in the area only a few miles distant from Mill View. They had arranged to meet at the club house for lunch.

He walked down to the garage and was backing out when, behind him, he caught sight of Mary in his mirror, waving her arms and blocking his path. He stopped, and there was the familiar smell of alcohol as she stuck her head in at the open window.

'Hello Mr High and Mighty! Trespassing again?'

'I can't back out of my garage any other way!' he said. 'There's not enough space. Surely you –'

'It's my land!' she shouted.

'Must go,' he said, continuing to reverse the big car slowly out of the garage. She was directly behind him, gesticulating and yelling insults, and he had a fleeting impulse to reverse over her. Instead, he swung the car round sharply and drove away up the lane with all possible speed. Bim will have to deal with her from now on, he thought. I don't trust myself not to flatten the bloody woman next time.

Over lunch, however, he forgot about Mary and such radical solutions. The food was excellent, the atmosphere agreeable, and he and his host had a long discussion about what the Bank of England was likely to do about interest rates and, a related issue, whether it was an opportune moment to make a bid for a competing company. (Thus bankrupting a rival and making a good profit simultaneously.) He felt himself relaxing as the comforting real world returned.

So it was a shock on his return to find that the landscape had changed outside his garage. Several quite large stones, almost boulders, had been placed in front of the two garages in such a way as to block his car's access, although not that of his neighbour. (Not that there was a car in that: it was full of junk.)

Clenching the steering wheel, Fraser swore violently. He could see tatty lace curtains moving, and knew he was being watched. He left the car, walked over to the little porch and rapped at the front door as hard as he could. But although he knocked and banged and rang the bell ferociously, nobody appeared – except Bim, who had heard the commotion from the garden.

'I'll do those,' Bim said, glancing at the stones.

'I'll wring that bloody woman's neck! Throw them in the bloody mill pond!' Fraser said. 'Get the council to clear it – I am being denied access to my own garage!' And he strode up the lane to his front gate.

Fraser rarely lost his temper and when he did, the idea that he had lost control, been at the mercy of his feelings and momentarily exposed, unsettled him. He tried to put it out of his mind and failed. Pleasure at the promising discussion at lunch, not to mention the prospect of outwitting a rival while making a profit, evaporated. He felt tired and irritable and did not sleep well that night. In the morning, however, the obstruction outside the garage appeared noticeably diminished. *Had* Bim manhandled some of the stones into the pond? When asked he just smiled and said he had 'arranged' them, and now there shouldn't be a problem. Fraser frowned, muttering, 'Bloody well better not be.'

For the next two months, Fraser was entirely taken up by FFG (Fraser Finance Global). He made business trips to South Africa, New Zealand, Indonesia, Hanoi, Singapore. The UK seemed very far away and indeed, if ever Mill View surfaced in his mind briefly, he realised that his initial satisfaction at acquiring his lost childhood home had somehow diminished. Perhaps 'going back' was always bound to end in disappointment.

As the summer faded, however, there was a lull in the world's fast-moving financial scene and, probably because of the series of highly lucrative deals he had negotiated during the past two months, he had largely forgotten about the petty irritations at Mill View and decided to make a visit. Bim, who recently seemed to have developed more of a will of his own, said he would prefer to defer his visit until the end of the week as he was over halfway through a course in Advanced Cordon Bleu Cookery. Put out, Fraser decided nevertheless to make a quick visit and Bim would join him a few days later.

September at Mill View was usually a beautiful month. Often very warm at that time of year, the mill pond always became unusually full because of autumnal high tides, water sometimes creeping up right across the road.

'Yes, sir, them old places down on the creek there, they flood regular come the autumn tides,' the publican said. 'Fred Olson had a great stack of sandbags by the front door, but I never heard as it kept him dry.'

'It can't affect me,' Fraser said. 'Mill View is higher up the lane.'

'Don't count on it,' the publican said.

Fraser's plane was delayed, and he was tired when he arrived by taxi late in the evening and went straight to bed. So did not see the three or four new boulders blocking access to his garage until the following morning. Still in his dressing gown he phoned Bim and told him that he must join him at Mill View immediately, otherwise he didn't know what he might do. Bim arrived four hours later, having driven without stopping once.

'I'll talk to her,' he said.

'*Talk* to her?'

'Arrange things,' Bim said. 'Don't worry.'

'I'm not worried,' snapped Fraser, breathless with anger. 'Ring the council again!'

Leaving the car behind this time, Bim returned to his cookery course having, with some difficulty, got rid of at least two of the stones – thus providing diagonal, rather skew-whiff access to the garage. He had also persuaded the still fuming Fraser to leave the matter for his London solicitor to solve and, above all, to calm down. Why not spend the few days before Bim's return playing golf, for instance? He made a few more sensible suggestions and then took the train back to London.

It was a perfect September, everything washed in the golden varnished light of early autumn. At high tide the huge mass of water from the estuary flooded in, creeping higher and higher across the road every evening. Low tide was equally extreme, revealing much of the muddy shoreline normally under water; seabirds followed the incoming tide, their cries and mournful piping echoing across the water. There was nobody about – except his neighbour, of course, who Fraser ignored. In spite of the good weather, it was now that he found himself thinking: 'Actually, what am I doing in this godforsaken muddy creek, when I could be in a villa in Capri or the south of France?' As a child he had sloshed along at the edge of the water at low tide, picking up unlikely treasure, and been happy. Once he had found part of a clay pipe, and another time a sodden wooden box containing a threepenny bit which flashed silver in the sun when polished. But these days mudlarking no longer appealed, and he had not been sleeping well: niggling anxieties about the huge new financial responsibilities he had shouldered in the past months seeped into his dreams and woke him. When Bim is not here I need a dog, he thought vaguely. I should take more exercise.

The footpath along the edge of the creek which he remembered from childhood was still there, and after a couple of bad nights he decided to wear himself out by walking up to the village and back. It was not far, even if some of the stiles had disintegrated and the bramble had grown almost impassable in places. However, he enjoyed the walk, and returning the same way saw that it was going to be an extra high tide this evening. The effort of walking and negotiating the overgrown path for a beer at the pub had relaxed him a little. But the moment he came up onto the road, frustration and resentment engulfed him at the sight of those damned boulders! Had she some-how put them back or added another one? Why hadn't the council acted? He stood, debating whether to go and bang on the cottage door again. Telephone the police? Bim? He could hear the familiar clamour of gulls following the advancing tide at the water's edge: they were making quite a racket and he wondered again how far it would come in tonight. It was several moments before he realised, suddenly, that what he was hearing was not a gull but a human voice.

'Help!' It was so faint that it was easy to mistake for a gull, or gulls. He listened and this time heard it quite clearly: 'H-e-l-p!'

Fraser walked onto the quay and looked over the edge. Mary was down there, half-leaning against the jetty wall and groaning, the rest of her splayed out on the soft mud. She looked a mess: face muddy and hair on end, one leg twisted under the other, her set of teeth and one bedroom slipper lying in the mud in front of her.

Drunk, he thought, coldly. Serves her right. Her own fault entirely, and he certainly wasn't going to climb down there into the mud and get filthy on her account. He turned away, ignoring the small voice whispering, 'How deep does it get down there at high tide? Help her, she's old.'

Damned if I lift a finger, he thought. She'll get herself out if she has to, bloody woman.

The phone was ringing as he walked into the house. It was Bim: did he realise he had missed a dental appointment?

'No, I didn't. Better get me another one,' Fraser said. 'See you.'

He had thought of booking a taxi to drive him to a 'Fine Dining' place tonight but in the end decided against it – he was not in the mood. He would make do with whatever he could find in the fridge, have a shower and then go to bed early. But first he needed a drink. The big open fire was already laid, logs stacked beside it. Fraser watched as the flames shot up, lighting the room with a flickering orange light. It soon began to warm up, and he sat back with his tumbler of whisky refilled, watching the flames. The whisky was a particularly good one – Bim had stocked the fridge with a large range of Fortnum's 'Country House Treats' – and there was an interesting documentary on the TV. Everything in the garden was perfect – or nearly perfect. Residual anxiety about the last deal in which he had been involved gnawed at him a little: investors can be so tricky. And the image of that scarecrow figure in the mud didn't help. For God's sake, that wretched woman! What had he done to deserve her? At the same time, how high did the water actually rise during these very high tides? Although there is nothing I can do now, he thought, it's well after eight o'clock. Resolutely he put it out of his mind until he had eaten, but then, unable to settle, fetched a jacket and walked down the lane.

It was getting dark, the moon's sad face rising from behind the further shore. He had been intending to walk right on to the little quay to make sure that . . . Well, just to make sure. But he saw at once that a huge sheet of water now stretched from across the far side of the creek, right up to his neighbour's front door and probably into both garages. Nothing I can do now, he thought again . . . I'll phone Bim. Unusually there was no reply, and he left a message to ring him back, poured himself more whisky and sat down in front of the fire, annoyed that Bim could not be contacted. He tried to relax and think calming thoughts, but failed; turned to *The Times* crossword but could not concentrate. He phoned Bim again several times, but he was either not there or not answering his mobile for some reason. I'm tired, he thought, and drank some more whisky. Very soon he went to bed.

Once in bed, he lay for a long time staring at the invisible ceiling and tossing about restlessly. Either the moonlight shining through the curtains, or perhaps the unpleasant images hovering on the edges of his mind, prevented sleep. But Fraser was nothing if not stubborn, and he must have been *trying* to sleep for a couple of hours when suddenly he sat up, conscious that he could hear something that sounded like water somewhere. The room was bright with moonlight, and he got out of bed to check the shower and taps in his bathroom; examined the ceiling for leaks or drips, but everything seemed as usual. Where was it coming from? He pulled back the curtains and at first did not recognise the scene beyond. The noise he had heard was water slapping up against the wall some little way down below his window. Silently, the tide had crept up the lane and now a solid sheet of moonlit water stretched from under his bedroom windows, over the road and the hedge, the little quay and jetty, to the further shore. If it rose much higher, his bedroom would start flooding.

How high was it going to get? He remembered the publican's comment: 'I wouldn't count on it!' Then, as he stood there watching, he caught sight of something that momentarily froze his heart. More or less at the spot where the small quay projected out into the mill pond – now under water but exactly where he had seen Mary sitting in the mud – he thought he saw a hand reaching up above the surface. Don't be ridiculous, he thought, you're imagining things – it's a branch, a bit of debris from the beach. But half a minute later, he saw it again quite clearly and it was definitely a hand, this time clawing at the air and waving frantically. With a single strangled cry, hands at his throat, choking, Fraser fell back onto the bed – and woke. It was a dream of course. A nightmare.

He did not fall asleep again until first light, and in the morning woke late, exhausted. Looking out of the window, he could see at a glance that the tide was now out; and after several cups of strong coffee, he walked down to the jetty and onto the quay. To his relief, there was nothing to be seen except a few gulls picking in the mud and some innocuous mounds of weed. The little quay looked as it always did; the cottage behind was quiet – but that was quite usual as Mary lived mainly in the kitchen at the back. When he returned to the house, there was a message from Bim to say, that he would be finishing his course tonight and planned to drive to Mill View tomorrow. Fraser immediately texted back – 'Make it tonight!' – and left a voicemail as well to be sure Bim got the message one way or another.

The day passed uneventfully enough, although he found it difficult to settle to anything. There had been no message from Bim, the atmosphere emanating from his dream of the previous night hung about like a bad smell, and he kept getting unsettling images of hands reaching towards him wherever he looked. He went for a walk to get some fresh air, flicked through the backlog of correspondence he had brought with him, read the latest financial news online and from time to time glanced out at the mill pond to see what the tide was doing. Very far out today, but what about tonight? I should know that sort of thing by now he thought, irritated – for God's sake, I grew up here! Finally he left a message for Bim to ask what time he was arriving tonight, and received an infuriating text by return. Bim had discovered that he had to show up on the last day of the course because otherwise he might not receive his diploma – the reason why he was doing the course in the first place. Fraser telephoned him back immediately, but Bim remained adamant.

'Don't worry, I've decided to fly. I'll be with you for breakfast!' he said cheerfully.

Fraser felt more unsettled than ever. What nonsense, he thought. I give him everything he could possibly want, why does he need a diploma?

Lying in bed later, for some reason memories of childhood crowded into his mind: the hot slates of the path leading from the gate, smell of the sea as it poured in over the mudflats, his weeping distraught mother and the confusion and tumult as they left the only home he had known. It hurt to think about it, but he could not stop. And last night? The water slapping against the wall under his window? Alright, it was a dream. But today he found it impossible to separate dream from reality and remained restlessly awake. How high would it get tonight? Surely the water must be receding by now?

Drawing back the curtains in a sudden gesture of defiance, and at first dazzled by the colourless brilliance of the moonlight, he saw with a jolt that the water had crept in over the little quay and the road below again, and now stretched from beneath his windows to the far edge of the creek, even higher than last night. He stared at it disbelievingly, and then drew in his breath sharply. He saw – *saw* – what he had seen last night: a hand reaching up out of the water – although tonight it was much closer. Close enough for him to see the separate fingers and chipped red nail varnish, the crooked beckoning index finger. Fraser drew the curtains together quickly and got back into bed; lay there waiting, rigid with apprehension. He had no idea what he was waiting for, although when there was a tap on the window and then another, he was not really surprised and knew at once that he must not on any account draw back the curtains. This is not *happening*, he told himself firmly again and again, it is all imagination. Nobody is tapping on the window out there, *nobody*! But he did not get up to look.

Fraser was still in bed with the curtains drawn when Bim arrived early the next morning. He was unnaturally pale and seemed uncharacteristically agitated and incoherent. Bim could get no sense out of him and called a doctor, fearing that Fraser had suffered a stroke. The doctor checked him over and said it was not a stroke, although Fraser's heartbeat was dangerously high and he didn't seem well at all. He advised Bim to call an ambulance at once. A private ambulance equipped with a paramedic was arranged, and with Bim sitting beside him Fraser was driven back to London and admitted to the London Clinic.

From then on, no doctor that Bim talked to had an adequate explanation of what was wrong with Fraser, although it was obvious that something serious had happened. Visiting him the next day, Bim saw that his hair had turned completely white – which rather suited him. By now he was in a clinic for nervous disorders and the consultant here could only say that unfortunately the blood pressure and high heart rate were still cause for concern; and that the patient was clearly highly disturbed and in a delusional state. Had there been some trauma or a bad experience recently? The patient was hallucinating and hysterical, convinced that he was in the water struggling with something or someone who was trying to kill him. For the moment, the best they could do was sedation and keep him under observation. Was there any history of insanity in the family?

In fact, Fraser lasted about a month after that. The sedation had been reduced at the end of the third week, and within a couple of hours he was madder than ever, screaming about 'That thing in the water! Look! Can't you see?' Then in the afternoon, he died.

Bim packed up Fraser's things, had an expensive sandwich and coffee at the clinic's restaurant, and took a taxi home.

After the funeral, the long tedious business of probate began. Bim managed it all with his usual efficiency – indeed seemed to be enjoying it. Apart from a modest bequest to his sister, Fraser had left everything to him, including Mill View – which he sold at once. He had never liked the place. With the figures for Mill View included, it all added up to an astonishing amount of money. Millions. When he was sure that it was all safely lodged, impeccably legal and all *his*, he leaned back in his chair, gave a big sigh of relief and began to plan how he was going to spend it.

Pink Hills

W hat was the matter with the planning department, Peter thought crossly as he closed his office door. Sandy soil, sloping ground and not far from the river? Any fool knew that deep excavation beneath buildings or gardens in that sort of terrain was asking for trouble. Anyway, why did the new owners of 41 Clegg's Road, the house opposite his own, *want* swimming pools, squash courts or whatever it was they intended to install under a large but perfectly ordinary suburban property? Were they going to dig out the whole of that beautiful garden? Mad . . . Well, *immoral*! He stuffed the planning application back in his pocket. Bea had wanted 41 because of the garden. Oh well, it doesn't matter now, he thought.

In order that a soothing measure of time should elapse between the office and the rigours of visiting his mother, he had decided to take the bus. Today, of course, it appeared almost immediately, taking him by surprise and rattling along at such a breakneck speed that he arrived at the door of her small terraced house almost before he had sat down.

The carer who opened the door seemed a pleasant, polite enough woman, although he knew that as a matter of principle his mother detested all the carers and nurses he managed to find. He walked upstairs to her bedroom – or bedsitting room as it had become. She was awake, sitting up in bed, glaring at him.

'Hello, who's that?'

'Me, Peter.' He moved the tray from the armchair and sat down.

'Oh! I thought Beatrice was coming today. What time is it?'

'Five past six.'

'In the morning?'

'Evening.' He examined her tray. 'Have you had tea?'

'No. Nobody's been here all day. I don't know where that woman is, that nurse? I am alone all the time.'

'The carer? She's downstairs.'

'She's got to go,' his mother said. 'I am not having anyone arranging things behind my back, interfering with my arrangements. It's like a boarding house. I don't want my spare room rented out like a cheap –'

'It is not rented out, Mother. The carers are sleeping in there. They have to sleep somewhere!'

How had Bea coped with his mother? She had been so good with her, good at everything, except at staying alive. Firmly, he said: 'Mother, you know you have to have someone with you –'

'Oh, don't go into all that again.'

'I know, but –'

'It is because I've been so careful, looked after my money and bought this house when I did, that I am in such a good position now.' She closed her eyes.

Bedridden, angry, mind slipping away like lumps of melting snow in a fast-flowing river, she lay back on the pillow. Surreptitiously he glanced at his watch. Only six-thirty, another hour to go. Six to seven-thirty, Mondays and Thursdays, that's what he and his conscience had agreed. His two older sisters divided up the rest of the week and coped alternate weekends. They do the bulk of it, he thought. I should be grateful.

'You look as if you are in mourning,' Mrs Jenner remarked suddenly. 'Has someone died?'

'I've come straight from the office, Mother. I have to wear a dark suit for work.'

There was a pause, into which his mobile shrilled suddenly.

'Dad? Minty has climbed out of the bathroom window and we can't get her back.'

'Cats are good climbers. She'll be OK. Leila, there's a pizza in the fridge – '

'Is it vegetarian?'

'Yes, no, I don't know. Anyway, put it in the oven at seven-thirty will you please? I'll be back at eight. Is Ben there?'

'On your computer, buying trainers.'

'Back soon.' He put his mobile back in his pocket.

His mother was asleep. Leaning back in his chair, he studied the worn, ivory-coloured, bone-thin old face. Like some pale fine stone blasted back to its essence by centuries of wind and rain. He felt himself relaxing.

'Pity I've lived so long,' Mrs Jenner said suddenly in a sharp loud voice, startling him. 'Saved everyone a lot of trouble if I had died by now. Isn't it time you were going?'

'Yes, I should make a move in a little while,' he said.

'How are the twins? Tell Beatrice I'd like a visit.'

'Yes'. He smiled at her. I haven't the energy to explain it again, he thought.

★

Slumped in his seat, he sat gazing out of the window of the bus: suburban villas in their sooty gardens, several garages — unsold cars cluttering the forecourts — greengrocers, one or two run-down cafés, builders merchants, pet shop, he knew it all by heart. But then, as it halted again in a particularly narrow stretch of road, he found himself gazing across the ten feet or so of pavement at a large painting, a landscape. It was propped on an easel, spotlit and positively glowing in the dusk, the only object in the window of what looked like an empty shop. A vision, he thought, pressing his face against the glass. Beautiful . . . He was still gazing at it as the bus moved off.

The pizza was burnt when he got home. Nevertheless, nine-tenths of it had been consumed, and although the twins, Leila and Ben, had now vanished, there was plenty of evidence that they had been around. 'And they've gone and opened my burgundy,' he muttered, holding up the bottle.

Leila came into the room deep in conversation on her mobile. She was wearing a tightly fitting black T-shirt cleft almost to the navel, a long lacy feather boa, black shorts and tights, pale thigh-length leather boots.

'Hi Dad! We had supper –'

'And helped yourself to my wine, I see?' Ignoring this remark, Leila continued her conversation.

'Leila!'

'Hang on, my Dad's talking to me . . . What? *What wine?* That was Ben – and his mate. Patrick told them not to.'

'Where are they now?'

'Playing snooker at the Cock and Feathers.'

'Is Patrick with them?'

'Probably. It's nothing to do with me –'

'Leila, you and Ben are still only sixteen –'

'Seventeen in two months!'

'Under age, and anyway I don't like the idea of Patrick – even if he is your cousin – or Ben and his friends, or you, opening my wine.'

'I don't like wine. It was Ben.'

'And the three of you have left a hell of a bloody mess. What's wrong with loading the dishwasher?'

Leila yawned. 'It's Ben's turn. I'm late, Dad. Babysitting at the Berrymans –'

'Dressed like that?'

'Like *what?*'

Leave it, he thought. 'Back here by eleven latest, please. And Leila, when I say eleven –'

'O-*KAY!* Heard you the first time.' Leila made for the door, mobile clamped to her ear, then halted. 'Dad, don't shut the bathroom window upstairs. Minty – the *cat!* Remember? Out on the flat roof?'

She talks to me as if I am mentally deficient, thought Peter, shoving the small sliver of burnt pizza into the bin. Not for the first time, he wondered how Bea would have coped with Leila.

He poured out the remainder of the burgundy and took a sip. Quite good, he thought, transferring the remains of the hunk of cheddar on the table to a tray, and taking out some pickle and half a 'sun-drenched olive rustic boutique' loaf from the fridge. This will do, I am too tired – and old – for bloody pizzas anyway. He put the bread and cheese, some apples and the jar of pickle, a bar of chocolate, on a tray with his glass, opened another bottle of burgundy and set off for the study. He was halfway up the stairs when the phone in the hall rang.

'Peter?' It was his sister Margo.

'If you want Patrick he is out.'

'How's Ma?'

'Much as usual.'

'But all right?'

'I suppose so.'

'How's the carer situation?'

'Expensive.'

'That's what worries me. Are you still adamant about a nursing home? She can afford it – well, she can if the house is sold.'

'You know what I think about that.'

'It might be the best option?'

'She'd hate it.'

'She hates it now –'

'I'm not putting Ma into a home, Margo. Look, I am tired, and –'

'Have you got another cleaner yet?'

'No –'

'Well, it will be the weekend soon. Tell Patrick to ring me. Kids OK?'

'Fine . . . when I see them.'

'You ought to be firmer – especially with Leila.'

'I know –'

'Well, don't let it get to you,' she said as she rang off.

There was a note from Ben on his desk: 'Nike Air Max only £300 on Ebay! Shall I get three pairs? Benjamin.'

It was cold upstairs. He shut the bathroom window, turned on the television and settled into his armchair with a large glass of wine.

He was loading the dishwasher when Leila got back, only ten minutes late.

'There are squatters over the road. Have you fed Minty?'

'No.'

'Where is she?' Leila disappeared up the stairs, reappearing a few minutes later with a large overweight tabby in her arms. 'Honestly, Dad! She was locked out on the bathroom roof, poor thing. She could have been there all night'.

'Cats like being on roofs,' he said. 'What was that about squatters? Where?'

'Opposite. Forty-one – great, isn't it?'

'Ah,' Peter said, feeling a warm glow of guilty satisfaction. 'Well, there's certainly room over there. Now, while I remember, I want you to visit Gran the Saturday after next. Both the aunts are away and –'

'Do I have to?'

'Yes, and Ben should go too.'

'Ben will be at Sophie's.'

'Leila, does Sophie's mother know about Ben?'

'Know what?'

'That they are –'

'What?'

'That they sleep together?'

'Oh God, *I* don't know. Dad, have we got anything we could lend them? Pillows? Blankets?'

'Lend who?'

'The squatters.'

'Certainly not –'

'What about that old telly in your study?'

'Go to bed, Leila.'

He was sitting at the kitchen table writing out another advertisement for a cleaner when his nephew Patrick and Ben walked in.

'Why are you so late?'

'It's not late. Any food? I'm starving,' Ben said.

Patrick is useless, he thought, standing by the window of his office the following day, yawning. Last night's conversation with his nephew had kept him awake.

'Patrick, the arrangement is that while you are here, you get your room rent free in return for being a responsible adult who stands in for me when I am late home. I really don't expect you to open my burgundy and then take Ben and his friend to the local pub. They are under age and –'

'It's not my fault your kids are out of control, and I didn't open your burgundy, it was Ben. Anyway, I won't be here much longer. I've decided to move in with Hermione.'

'Move? When?'

'Next week?'

'Next *week*?'

'Hermione's idea.' He paused. 'Peter, you need to do something about Ben. It was his suggestion that we open the wine, and it isn't just me he goes to the pub with. As for Leila, she's –'

'So your mother is always telling me. She rang you, by the way.'

After the shock of Patrick's defection and a protracted battle over the trainers, the weekend went rather better than usual. Saturday passed without the usual arguments about homework or coursework or whatever they called it nowadays, and on Sunday morning Leila, unusually, made a very delicious chocolate cake. Never mind that the sink and draining board were crammed with mixing bowls and saucepans, grated chocolate trodden up the stairs, it was good that she took an interest. And now, both she and Ben had gone off somewhere, so he had time to himself – which should please me, he thought. Instead, such a pall of loneliness and inertia descended, it seemed almost physical. Pull yourself together, he muttered. *Do* something . . . Go for a walk! Why didn't he want to?

On Sundays, the broad walk beside the river ten minutes' walk away was usually busy, and so it was today. Children on scooters swooped among the rows of skiffs; gaggles of young men carrying oars stood together gossiping, couples with push chairs, toddlers and babies in slings ambled along. A relaxed and charming scene which, today, completely failed to charm him. I am getting old, he thought.

As he walked towards the swans, he noticed someone he had seen down here before: a tall statuesque lady in a flapping brightly-coloured skirt, now wobbling unsteadily towards him on a bicycle, balancing a large basket of shopping on her handlebars. Smiling and teetering precariously, she cycled past him, untidy mass of hair blowing in the wind. Basket too big and skirt too long, he thought, expecting to hear a crash as she disappeared behind a group of pensioners feeding the swans. Sighing, he reflected that the usual magic of the river was not working. Back home, Leila's chocolate cake, to which he had been looking forward, was nowhere to be found.

Sitting in his mother's room the following evening, he remembered Trollope's observation that the capacity to be disagreeable is the characteristic which remains with us longest in life.

'We've got squatters over the road,' he said conversationally.

'Squatters? Sounds like me!' Mrs Jenner replied crisply.

'Mother! Residential nurses and carers with no address near must have somewhere to sleep on their nights off,' he said wearily.

'They could go home!'

'To New Zealand? They have to sleep somewhere.'

'Don't keep saying that.' Painfully she struggled upright, 'Loretto? *Loretto?*'

'I think her name is Carlotta'.

'Lotto,' his mother repeated as the carer entered the room with more hot water. 'What was it I was going to ask my son?'

Carlotta smiled, shaking her head, and did not answer the question.

'Lotto's lost her memory.' His mother's sardonic grin unnerved him.

'I am sorry she is so difficult,' he said when Carlotta met him in the hall with his briefcase.

'It is hard for her. But hard for you too,' she said. 'Perhaps you should try and give yourself a break sometimes?'

In the bus on the way home he thought, if I start having 'breaks' I am lost! Champagne at breakfast, walking in the Himalayas, scuba diving on the Great Barrier Reef, dancing girls, no children – no, I don't mean that. Since Bea died, he had had one or two passing flings, even tried a dating agency.

But the twins had reacted badly, after which he stopped trying. Recently, a divorced friend of Margo's who he'd fancied had shown an interest. But she had proved to be allergic to cats, particularly Minty, which didn't go down well with Leila. A spectacular falling-out between all parties ensued, and 'it' was over before it had begun. He was still ruminating on the conundrum of his life when the bus, which usually idled along this section of the High Street, halted abruptly and he caught sight of the painted landscape again, this time appearing almost luminous in the dark. He rang the bell and got off.

Close to, the landscape of hills and a distant sea was even more impressive. Jade and olive greens, dark purplish blue, transparent iridescent pink glazes, proceeding towards a distant skyline in fold after fold of dazzling colour. Unrealistic yet completely convincing – he had never seen anything like it.

'How much is this?' he asked the bored-looking girl who appeared from the back of the shop.

'It's a temporary display.' She looked at him without interest. 'Just there to fill in until the next exhibition.'

'How much?'

'I don't know if it's for sale. Not in the catalogue. Sorry.'

He wrote his phone number and name and address on a slip of paper, and gave it to her. 'Could you let me know, please?'

Waiting for the bus, the colours of the landscape glowed before his inner eye like a radiant calming vision. Why *don't* I give myself a break, he thought, smiling. A run-down little gallery like that couldn't charge much for its paintings, surely? But sitting in the bus a few minutes later, he had a disconcerting vision of Leila's incredulous face; remembered conversations with Ben about money and how it did not grow on trees. How could I possibly justify it, he thought. I am being ridiculous. We struggle as it is. On the other hand . . . We don't have a car ('What's a car got to do with it, Dad?'), and I hardly ever – well, *never* – buy anything for myself. He went seesawing on like this for the remainder of the bus ride.

The house was dark and cold when he got home, but there was a comforting aroma wafting up from the kitchen.

'Anybody at home?' he called. 'Something smells wonderful.'

Leila stood at the stove, stirring the contents of a large saucepan, while Ben had school work spread out over every inch of the kitchen table. A peaceful domestic scene.

'That smells delicious.' Peter took off his coat and looked into the pan. 'What is it?'

'Vegetarian goulash with herbs. Dad, Number Forty-one's water has been turned off. Can they come over here and have showers?'

'No, Leila.'

'Oh Dad! They can't get jobs, and because they can't earn they can't –'

'Perhaps that makes you realise how very privileged –'

'Adam's brother was at school with Patrick,' Leila said. 'He's a sociology graduate at Sussex.'

'How do you know?'

'He told me.'

'You mean you've been over there?'

'Ben and I were there on Saturday and Sunday helping them put a bed pack from Ikea together.'

'Ikea? They are not starving, then?'

'He can't get a job and he owes so much money on his fees he daren't do an MA. Do you want some of this?'

'I've bought a chicken korma, Dad.' Ben made a face behind Leila's back. 'Share it if you don't fancy vegetarian muck. Why is Patrick leaving?'

'He's decided to move in with Hermione.'

'Can Adam have his room then?' Leila asked immediately.

'No, Leila.'

'Why not?'

'I'm not discussing it. Next weekend – are you listening? I want you both to go and visit Gran.'

'You're not serious?'

'In the afternoon. Both of you. She needs cheering up and anyway, it's a long time since you –'

'I've got revision every weekend until the end of term,' Ben said quickly.

'You will have to curtail your social life on weekdays then, won't you?'

On Friday evening he raised the question of visiting Mrs Jenner again and a full-scale row with Leila erupted. And when a perfectly satisfactory middle-aged woman came to be interviewed about the cleaning job, she took one look at the kitchen and Leila's angry face and said she thought it would be too much for her.

'It's too much for me too!' he bellowed at the twins when she had gone. 'Tomorrow, you can both bloody well stay in and help me clean up!'

'I thought you wanted us to go and visit Gran?' Ben said from the kitchen floor, where he was slowly dismantling his bike.

'That's the afternoon. Ben, do you *have* to do that in here?'

'Where else is there?'

'Oh, Dad, someone rang you,' Leila said. 'About a paint-ing?'

'Yes?'

'She'll ring again.'

'What's the number?'

'I didn't have a pencil.'

It's like walking through treacle, he thought.

'You should pay us for doing this,' Leila said, pulling the vac-uum cleaner listlessly across the hall floor the following day. 'Cleaners get *pounds* –'

'Yes, because they do it properly and don't have to be bul-lied. And anyway, I never stop paying – your phone, for ex-ample.'

Ben opened the front door and then closed it again.

'Front steps are OK.'

'Leila, finish the hall, please, and yes, Ben, sweep the front steps and round the dustbins and then you can start upstairs.'

'But Patrick did all that yesterday!'

'Do it again. And pick up all the things on your floor, Ben.'

Ben leaned against the banisters as if he was about to be sick. 'My bedroom is my private space.'

'Tough.'

'It's so middle class, this cleanliness thing,' Leila muttered.

At three o'clock, the twins left to visit their grandmother. Surveying the kitchen – dishwasher emptied, floor vacuumed and clear of the usual muddle of trainers, baskets, recycling bags, tools, old milk bottles, remnants of Ben's bicycle – Peter felt a sense of achievement. Now for my 'break,' he thought.

He nearly walked past the place, sandwiched as it was between a betting shop and a greengrocer. It would be just like life – his life – if they had gone and sold it! No, it was still there, and when Peter asked the price he was agreeably surprised.

'Reduced,' the girl said. 'Seeing as how nothing sold.'

'

When he got home, he propped the painting up on the end of the kitchen table and sat for a long time gazing at it. If those two disapprove, he thought, that is just too bad. He was beginning to consider hanging spaces when the front-door bell rang. The twins without their keys? Someone selling something? Jehovah's Witnesses? It rang again. It must be the twins. He walked up the stairs rehearsing what he was going to say to them, each justification equally unconvincing.

A tall, vaguely familiar woman stood on the top step, smiling nervously.

'Oh, I'm sorry . . . Am I disturbing you?'

'No, it's fine – '

'I was visiting – er, in the road – and I just wanted to ask you –'

He knew her face, didn't he?'

'Actually, I phoned and left a message. I heard you were interested?'

'Interested?'

'In my landscape . . . *Pink Hills?*'

'That is *your* painting?' He realised, suddenly, where and when he had seen her. 'I am Peter Jenner, by the way.'

'Eleanor,' she said. 'Fahey.'

'I bought it!' He grinned. 'This afternoon.'

'Oh!'

'I have only been back from the gallery a few minutes. As you are here, why don't you come in? Help me hang it? I am just about to make a cup of tea.'

She had an attractive, somewhat diffident smile and was taller than him, hair coiled up on her head in untidy swathes. Close to, he saw pink unlined skin and large trusting hazel eyes.

'Haven't I seen you . . . down near the river? On a bicycle?'

'That's right. Your face is familiar too.' They both laughed.

In the kitchen she sat at the table, eyes turned towards the picture, while he poured the tea. 'Actually it looks . . . alright,' she said, sounding as if she had trouble believing this.

'Alright? It's *lovely*!'

'Thanks. I hadn't realised you had been in to the gallery again. I mustn't stay long, I am visiting my son.'

'Does he live near?'

'Opposite.'

'Oh, one of the squatters?'

'Temporarily. He has been sharing with me in my very small flat. But recently I have had my father staying – just out of hospital – and they don't get on.' Her expression was wry and a little sad. 'Do you have children?'

'A boy and a girl. Twins. They are out at present.' (Thank heavens, he thought.)

'Sons can be quite difficult, can't they?'

'So can daughters. Have some more tea? Cake's vanished, I'm afraid.'

They were still sitting in the kitchen chatting when the front door slammed upstairs, and after the usual racket of footsteps thumping across the hall and crashing down the stairs Leila walked into the kitchen with Ben close behind her.

'Dad!'

'We have a visitor, Leila. This is Eleanor.'

They glanced at her briefly and Ben muttered, 'Hi, Eleanor.' Leila, clearly in ecstasy about something, waved a slip of paper under his nose.

'Look! *Money!*'

'What? Why?'

'For visiting her and –'

'Cheering her up,' Ben said. 'Dad, I'm starving!'

'How is she?'

'OK. She –'

'She asked us to come again, bring our friends,' interrupted Leila.

'What friends?'

'People,' Leila said, glancing towards Eleanor as if she had just caught sight of her. 'Hi! Are you the new cleaner?'

'Leila, this is Eleanor,' Peter said again quickly.

'We took Adam and Dan with us –'

'And?'

'They got on like a house on fire. Adam hates the banks as much as Gran! For different reasons, of course,' Leila added.

'Yeah. Really cool.' Ben nodded. 'Dad, is there any food? I'm –'

'Gran's not like you, Dad. More open-minded,' Leila interjected. 'Adam played his guitar and Dan told her jokes –'

'*I* told the jokes,' Ben interrupted. He pointed at the landscape shimmering at the end of the table. 'What is *that*?'

Leila swivelled round to stare at the canvas. 'Yes, what *is* that?'

'*Pink Hills*. I've just bought it.'

'What?'

'The painting. I've just bought it.'

'*Bought?*' they echoed in unison.

'Yes –'

'Bought a *picture*,' whispered Leila.

'Yes, painted by Eleanor here . . . Adam's mum. I think it's beautiful.'

Nobody spoke for a moment.

'Wow! How cool is that,' Ben said faintly.

Leila gazed first at her father, then at Eleanor.

'You are Adam's mum?'

Eleanor nodded and put out a hand to stroke Minty, who had jumped up onto the table and was stretching herself full-length in front of the canvas.

'Hello, beautiful,' she said. 'What's your name?'

'Do you have a cat?' Leila asked.

'I have two'.

'Two! Dad will only let me have one! What are they?'

'Persian Blue – crossed with Siamese.'

'Minty is Burmese crossed with – well, mostly tabby. Actually I quite like your painting.'

'Good,' Eleanor said, stroking the purring Minty behind the ears.

'Did you say you were on your way to visit Forty-one?' Peter asked suddenly.

'Yes, I should go.'

'Leila, why don't you ask Adam and his friend over?'

Leila stared at her father for a moment, frowning.

'*Here?* You mean – OK, I'll text him.'

'We'll get a pizza delivered and celebrate! It's not every day I buy a painting.' Peter smiled at Eleanor. 'Do stay? I'll open a bottle of wine, and you can help us decide where we should hang it.'

Leila handed Peter her mobile. 'Better order five or six pizzas, Dad. You know what Ben is like, ravening wolves down on the fold or whatever!'

It was much later in the evening when Peter banged in a few rawlplugs over the mantelpiece in his study, and they all stood back to admire Eleanor's painting. The landscape seemed to glow, pulse, radiating light into the room like an extra dimension.

'Sort of bright . . . Better on the wall,' Ben said, glancing at Leila.

'Bright? It's psychedelic!' she said. Next to her, Adam laughed.

'And all done by hand!'

Peter studied the painting, head on one side. 'But is it the right height? What do you think?'

'I think it's like, awesome!' Leila said, looking first at Eleanor and then her father and bursting into laughter. 'Cheers, Dad!'

Civil War

I t is a strange thing, being in that house,' my brother said. 'The guns, just left around. And his things all over the place: clothes, books, even shaving brushes. Sometimes I get the feeling . . . Well, that he might just walk in.'

'But he is not living there now?'

'No.'

'What would happen?'

'I don't know. He's a tough man, a hunter . . . accustomed to killing, as it were.'

'Is Mariella afraid of him?'

'She told me there is nothing more frightening than be-ing alone in the house with a jealous man . . . and his guns,' my brother said. 'There's something –' He hesitated. 'Well, the whole family . . . Her brother-in-law has a collection of knives. It's a primitive country still, of course,' he added, as if explaining something to himself.

'What makes you think I'd enjoy it there? Although if you like it, I suppose I will?'

Being twins, Sam and I are very close, share many tastes.

I cannot now remember what the answer was; something about my lonely state, recent car accident, needing a holiday? Anyway I must have been convinced. I booked the flight the same afternoon – to follow him out in a month's time.

I had an oddly complete picture of the house in my mind before I actually saw it: the colour, smell, feel. Wood, wood smoke perhaps? An impression of shadow, space. Told by Sam that the upper floors, indeed much of the house, were unused and empty, I filled it. With what, I am not sure. Some kind of pleasurable menace.

We were delayed at the airport; trouble ahead in the queue. But I was in holiday mood. Anything was preferable to sitting in my flat alone, or in front of a class of bolshie fifteen-year-olds. Teaching is not really what I wanted to do in life, and anyway, since my car accident I seem to feel different about a lot of things, airports included.

In the plane waiting our turn on the runway, the woman sitting next to me said suddenly:

'What about those Cubans? Did you see? They had a dip-lomatic bag.'

'Cubans?'

'Yes, that man, the black one. That's why there was a delay. Did they put the diplomatic bag on? What's in it, I wonder? My God, perhaps we'll be blown up?'

I looked at her. Expensive clothes, highlights, a sharp nose like a talon between dark glasses; innumerable bangles and chains clinking with every movement.

'Flying is dangerous nowadays. You can be sitting next to a terrorist!' The engines began to roar, preparing for take-off. 'This is a new plane, I hope they know how it works!'

When we were airborne I stared out of the window reso-lutely, then took out my book, and she must have lost interest or thought I was reading as she did not address me again until we were circling over the dusty palms and red roofs of our

destination. She leaned towards me lowering her voice con-
spiratorially.

'It's a terrible thing to say, but these people are happier with
a dictator. I am from Latin America myself, so I know.'

My legs had been pronounced mended but I still tired easily
and was inclined to limp, so I was grateful that Sam was at the
airport with a car, having taken time off the work he was supposed to be doing: he is an entomologist and makes a special
study of leaf miners in relation to horticulture. It happened to
be vineyards here, but it might just as well have been chrysan-
themums or potatoes in another part of the world. (Both Sam
and I took biology degrees, but it sometimes seems as if he has
made better use of it than I.)

I knew a little about Mariella, her history, her family and its
present circumstances, from Sam. They had been friends for
years, and he often stayed with her. But nothing had prepared
me for the sheer beauty of the woman who now came running
down the steps from the front door, was lost for a moment in
the courtyard and screen of trees, reappearing on the further
side of high iron gates: double gates, I noticed, both locked.
Lithe and graceful, with long silky brown hair and a skin
more like some sort of perfect fruit than flesh and blood, she
seemed imbued with a kind of freshness and intensity usually
present only in the very young. I would have said twenty-five
if asked her age. But Sam and she had been teenage sweet-
hearts and since then she had married and was the mother of a
grown-up son. She must have been at least forty.

The house itself was a surprise too. Obscured from the
casual passer-by by thickets of creeper and vine, immensely
tall sweet-smelling *Datura* trees, only the peeling stucco

façade and iron balcony in front of the first-floor windows could be glimpsed between the leaves, perhaps some of the upper floors. However, once through the gates and up to the gardens beyond, a greater contrast to the cacophonous graffiti-blasted streets outside would be hard to imagine. And in the fashionable suburb of a great city I had not expected what was, to me, a bizarre combination of calm elegance and farm-yard: vegetables, flowering trees, shrubs, the peaceful court-yard with its terracotta pots, strutting chickens and their droppings, geraniums, flights of stone steps, dogs too old now for hunting, lounging and scratching in the shade.

It was more as I had imagined inside the house, and I no-ticed the guns at once – on the walls of the entrance hall, in the dining room, up the stairs. But they looked like collec-tors' pieces to me: ornamental, historic. The narrow leather cases on top of various cupboards and tables on the ground floor were less reassuring. Sam and Mariella were laughing together.

'I have given you my room,' she said, turning to me. 'Sam's sister is an honoured guest!'

'You shouldn't have done that!' I was a little dismayed at the idea that she had turned out of her room, her bed. I cer-tainly would not have done the same if our positions had been reversed.

'It is an honour to give you hospitality! My room has a nice view from the balcony. Besides, I often sleep downstairs.' She pointed at a door behind me. 'In my little sitting room, with all my books. We are very simple now,' she added. 'Most of the house is shut up; things have become so expensive here, and we don't need all those rooms.' She laughed and tossed back her hair. She had beautiful white teeth, I noticed, but sad eyes. My brother obviously still found her very attractive, who would not? I wondered suddenly whether they were lovers again? It was some time since his marriage had ended. Perhaps that was why she had turned out of her bed? Sam seemed extraordinarily happy as the two of them stood together smiling at me. Too happy, I remember thinking later.

At dinner that first evening I met Mariella's son Vitor who, in some mysterious way, had been posted back with his unit at the end of its tour of duty and was billeted in his own home. Not enough room at the barracks, perhaps?

He was a grave straight-backed young man, very formal in his military uniform, with that perfect unblemished glow of youth which is at once so pathetic and so appealing. He was in fact twenty-three at that time, although he did not look much younger than his mother, whom he resembled greatly: dark hair but cropped very short, and the same pale light eyes fringed with black. Only his height and obvious physical strength, a certain brooding reserve, seemed altogether at odds with her grace and vitality. Whereas she smiled and laughed easily, chattering in English with my brother, Vitor remained silent, impassive, watching them as if at a distance. I thought he did not speak English, wrongly as it turned out.

An argument started between Mariella and my brother, good-tempered but intense nonetheless.

'Well, surely you agree,' Sam was saying, 'that a colonial war is a terrible and unnecessary drain? It is a good thing it's over and your people are coming back now.'

'You are talking like my husband' – this was Mariella. 'He would like to fill this house with beggars . . . anybody. Have you seen the shanty towns? There's nothing for them here – prices going up all the time, no work and now these new trade-union laws.'

She shrugged, glancing at her son. 'Vitor too. Ask him. It's what he and his friends want.'

'What do you think, Vitor?' my brother asked.

'The same as my father,' the young man replied after a pause. 'The country has to move forward.'

Mariella shook her head sadly. 'But innocent people are being arrested, Vitor. Your cousin has been in prison for two months. And what about elections? There will be civil war if there are no elections.'

'We exist in a climate of civil war as it is, Mamma,' he replied, smiling faintly. 'You are living in the past.'

There was a brief hiatus in the conversation; as if deliberately he had dropped his plate on the floor, spat at someone. Mariella seemed embarrassed.

'You will never convince her,' Sam said lightly. 'She's a counter-revolutionary by nature.' He laughed and began to talk, gently teasing; a diversion. I looked at Vitor more carefully. It occurred to me then that under that impassive exterior he was exceedingly angry.

My brother left for the north to continue with his work, leaving me at La Caicca with Mariella until his return in ten days' time. Then we planned to go off in the car to see a bit of the country, perhaps to the mountains.

It was very hot. I spent my time reading – my room was full of books – swam off the nearest beach, or went with Mariella to the market and then on to one of the dark little cafés down on one of the beaches for a stickily sweet thick black coffee laced with curaçao.

'What is your favourite book?' Mariella asked one morning when we were sitting together at the café on the square nearest the house. 'Mine is *Wuthering Heights* – and Apollinaire. You know him?'

'I don't read French, or not well enough.'

'Ah, I read it like a native. And then English, I am bilingual. And of course, my own language.'

'Like a native,' I said. She laughed and then sighed.

'*Wuthering Heights*,' she said again. 'I can identify, you see.'

I could understand that. Mariella, with her dark hair, pale skin, tempestuous nature, would be a perfect Cathy. I wondered about Heathcliff. As if she had read my thoughts, she said:

'My husband . . . He does not live with me, you know. We are divorced.' I nodded, not knowing quite what to say. I had thought of Mariella as a Catholic in a very Catholic country. 'Divorce is possible here, now.' Again I nodded sympathetically. 'I am a native, but I no longer belong. I should go, get out – God knows where. There is nothing for me in this country any more. I hate it.' She sipped her coffee without looking at me. 'It is hard for people like us. I am wondering whether we will get our wine made on the estate this year.'

I knew that Mariella's family had owned land, an estate and large farm, vineyards in the north, for generations, and remembered the woman on the plane.

'Big changes since your dictator went?'

'We didn't like him, of course, but things were stable; prices, food. And people worked. They had to. We only have

two men on our land now, working. That is why I am worried
about the wine. The others have gone.'

'What does your son feel about that? The wine?' I asked.
But Mariella pulled a face and did not reply.

Before dinner that evening I had a chance to talk or, rather,
listen to Vitor as we sat on the steps above the courtyard with
our vermouth. He spoke with all the vehement certainty of
youth. My brother's children are the same. Markedly similar
opinions too, I noticed.

'There must be changes for this country to survive eco-
nomically – and in every other way,' he said, gazing at the
purple banks of cloud gathering above the sea. 'The armed
forces are in the forefront of these changes, so we have the
right to decide what sort of direction.'

'What kind of changes?' I had heard this sort of thing before, in theory at least, from Sam's children.

'Power must be exercised by collective organs emerging from a democratic system, the economy planned. The
people must own their own natural resources, industries . . .
Mines, natural gas, oil.'

'Vineyards?'

'In some cases.' Vitor did not look directly at me. 'Yes,
vineyards too.'

'A people's democracy, perhaps?' I was getting bored.

He thought for a moment. 'There have to be changes. At
my father's hospital, he is a doctor –'

Again I interrupted him. 'What does your father feel?' I
knew Vitor was fond of his father, saw him regularly.

'My father is an idealist, an intellectual. He was very much
against the last government,' Vitor replied after a pause. His

face softened. 'My father is a good man. Very kind. Too kind, perhaps.'

I remembered the guns and wondered. Guns and idealism go together. But medicine?

'What sort of doctor is your father?'

'He works at the City Hospital, the people's hospital. Rheumatology.'

'He's a hunter too, is he?' Vitor gave me a sidelong unsmiling glance, put down his glass and stood up.

'No, not him. Please excuse me, I must help my mother.'

I wouldn't have thought much about it, except that the following day I saw Vitor with his father. They were sitting together at a small table in the square drinking cognac and smoking those thin astringent cigarillos that are so characteristic of the country.

I knew at once who it was, partly because Mariella had told me that Vitor was to see his father that afternoon: she had been excitable and strung up all day and I supposed that this was the reason; and partly because of two photographs I had seen. One, a framed wedding group in Vitor's room visible from the stairs: a touchingly young Mariella and her bridegroom: there was no doubt it was the same man; as was the subject of another photograph I found tucked into one of the books in Mariella's bedroom. *Paradise Lost* in Italian translation. This was a portrait study, head and shoulders only; a strong, powerful, very good-looking man with black unruly hair brushed loosely back from his forehead, dark Phoenician eyes, brows meeting above a jutting nose. I remember thinking that the middle-aged suited figure I had glimpsed in the square, face shaded and obscured by his hat, seemed ordinary enough. The man who gazed up from between the pages of *Paradise Lost* was altogether fiercer, rougher; somehow unsettling. At the time I assumed that it was a younger version of the man in the square, age having effected some sort of calming transformation.

I was tired and went up to my room early. Lights bobbed and winked in the streets beyond the trees and I stood by the window with the shutters pushed open, grateful for the cool air blowing in from the sea. Mariella's garden had been watered during the evening and a metallic mineral smell of damp earth mixed with the sweet smell of the *Datura* flowers filled the room. I watched a cat walk slowly across the courtyard below, jump onto the high wall enclosing the house, and spring away into the darkness on the further side of the gate through which now someone let themselves in: the gardener perhaps, or housekeeper's son? He lived with his parents as Vitor lived, at present, with his mother.

Mariella's room had its own small bathroom and shower, a cramped antiquated arrangement in a kind of tiled box room off to one side. I decided I would have a bath.

It was deliciously cool in there, several degrees lower than the bedroom. Before turning on the water I stood leaning against the wall, leafing through a folder of poems, translations, given to me by Mariella: some young poet, male of course, who she was encouraging. They were good, and I began to read more carefully, holding the pages up to the narrow shaft of light spilling through the half-open door; it had grown suddenly much darker and the switch was in the bedroom. As I stood there reading, some slight sound, subtle alteration in the domestic landscape, made me raise my eyes while keeping completely motionless. From where I stood in the shadow of the bathroom, part of a large ornately framed mirror hanging above the bed head was visible. In it, now, I saw the reflection of a man standing just inside the open window. He was leaning forward, balanced like a dancer, listening intently. I could only see his profile, but I knew at once who it was. Mariella's husband, ex-husband.

The image slipped from the mirror. I heard him moving about in the room, watched when he reappeared, not a reflection this time but a tall, powerfully-built man standing by the bedside table looking through the books I had left there. The light was shining full on his face; he was so close I could hear the intake of breath, examine the waxy texture of skin above where he shaved, black hair on the back of his hands, large strong fingers, spatulate nails beautifully formed. The smell of eau de cologne came to me faintly. Suddenly he laughed, and I realised he was holding up the photograph of himself that I had just tucked back into *Paradise Lost*. He was like the photograph and not like. Better looking, not so heavy, saturnine. Or perhaps it was just that standing only a few yards away one could sense the drive and magnetism more acutely? I thought he must turn and see me, feel the presence of another human being. But he merely replaced the photograph and the book, glanced quickly at the room behind him and opened the door to the landing. I was left standing against the wall of the bathroom, heart beating uncomfortably fast, wishing I had summoned up the nerve to say something to him.

The bedroom seemed unnaturally bright, lit as if by search-lights. I closed the windows, switched off all but one lamp, and went out onto the landing. As I stood there in semi-darkness, gazing at the glow from the chandelier in the hall two flights down, a door on the half landing below me opened and Vitor appeared. He did not look up but walked slowly down the stairs, stood for a moment outside Mariella's study door as if collecting himself, knocked and went in. Returning to my room mystified and uneasy, it occurred to me that – apart from tonight's visitor and whatever he was up to – there was some odd quality about the atmosphere of this house and its occupants difficult to analyse, which made me thoroughly uncomfortable.

I picked up *Paradise Lost* to look again at the photograph and as I did so heard a woman scream somewhere downstairs, whether in anger or fear I was not sure. I opened my door again and listened. The silent house had burst into life and clattered with a confused and confusing hubbub: running footsteps, a man's voice shouting, other voices raised shrilly as if driven beyond endurance. Reluctantly I walked downstairs, to find Mariella and Vitor in the hall facing each other like gladiators, he towering over his mother and haranguing her in a fierce angry voice apparently quite out of control. I wondered if he was drunk? Oblivious to me, and to the housekeeper who I now saw standing at the far end of the passage which led to the kitchen, Mariella screamed back. Not speaking the language, I understood nothing – except that they were both shockingly angry. Finally, after a crescendo of passion, Mariella stalked towards the front door, wrenched it open and swept out into the warm dark night.

'Vitor!' I exclaimed somewhat peremptorily. 'Your mother? What is happening?' I could smell cigar smoke and wondered suddenly if the husband, Vitor's father, was sitting in the little study listening to all this. Presumably he had expected to find Mariella in the room upstairs? Why on earth was he entering the house by an upstairs window? They were divorced – had he been forbidden the house, and she had insisted on leaving rather than face him? Vitor turned, apparently seeing me for the first time.

'Nothing,' he replied coldly. 'Nothing is happening, happens. Everything is normal, completely normal. My mother has decided . . . to go out. As you can see.' And with no further explanation he closed the front door and walked past me into the study. It's children quarrelling, I thought, mother-and-son stuff, and went back to my room.

The sun was already high when I woke late, unrefreshed. I had taken the precaution of locking shutters and windows the night before, and the room was hot and stuffy. From downstairs came the smell of freshly roasted coffee.

In the dining room I found Vitor alone, dressed as usual in his immaculate uniform, his handsome face expressionless. He rose as I entered the room, wiping his mouth with a napkin.

'Good morning. I am sorry to be so late.'

He gave a little bow. 'You will take coffee?'

'Thank you. And Mariella?' I asked. 'Has she had breakfast? That is, will she, er . . .' I floundered. Perhaps she had not come back after rushing out into the night? He stared at me with eyes exactly like his mother's.

'My mother is a law . . . Like you say, to herself a law. I do not know her plan . . . Plans. Please excuse me, I have to report to my commanding officer.' He bowed again, turned abruptly and left the room 'marching as if to war'. Why did I say that? I have often thought of it since.

★

It was already very hot, and I had a headache. I decided to stay in the cool, upstairs for a while, write some postcards to be posted later in the day. But Mariella's absence and the events of the previous evening made me restless. I began to prowl about her room, picking up books – in which I found more photos, all of the same man – opening cupboards, even lifting the heavy pewter candlesticks from the top of a chest at the foot of the bed in order to look inside.

It was deep, capacious, smelt of some aromatic herb and had been packed full of linen and folded lengths of cloth, pieces of brocade. I lifted out some of the sheets and table cloths, napkins, lace-edged pillow slips, in order to look at an embroidered cushion beneath, and remained transfixed. At the bottom of the chest, stacked neatly one on top of another, were a number of very lethal-looking guns of varying sizes. I know nothing about arms of any kind. I have never shot anything, not even rabbits or at a fair. But even I knew, perhaps from television, that these were not some amateur's cast-off collection but modern, up-to-date automatic weapons meant for killing people. I wondered if there was ammunition in there as well. Was this what my brother meant by 'guns all over the house'? It was surprising that the chest had not been locked.

The front door slammed downstairs and I thought it must be Vitor leaving. Then I heard the dogs barking and Mariella's voice. I replaced the lengths of cloth, cushion, the linen, and closed the chest quickly. When Mariella's knock came I was lying on my bed – her bed – with my eyes closed.

'You are tired?' she asked, coming to perch beside me. 'Did you not sleep well? I must apologise for not being here at breakfast. I was at Mass . . . Did Vitor look after you? He is stupid sometimes, he gets so angry with his mother!' She laughed merrily and patted my arm. 'Dear Vitor! I love him . . . He tries to protect me. But I am difficult.'

I lay back on the pillows and studied the face above mine. Any trace of the ferocity of the night before had vanished. She was clear-eyed, animated, her cheeks pink and glowing.

'I prayed to the Virgin for your complete recovery, your poor legs!' She laughed again. I wondered if she knew what was in the chest.

Mariella was disarming, there was no doubt about that. I sat in the kitchen watching her make coffee and debated whether to say anything. Difficult to admit that I had been poking about amongst her possessions. Finally I said: 'The guns in this house, Mariella, do they frighten you? I mean, do you keep them locked away, mostly?'

'Guns?' She sounded vague. 'I don't like them but what can I do? In this country everyone has them. Everyone, everywhere. Politics and guns in everything. It makes trouble.' I said nothing and she continued: 'My husband and Vitor are wrong about politics. Both of them.'

'What sort of politics?' I asked, meaning to go back to the guns later.

'He gets so angry, but –' At this point the telephone rang and Mariella left the room to answer it. She was away a long time and I suppose I could have dropped it, changed the subject, but I wanted to know about this husband who walked in and out of the house through the windows at night. It might happen again, after all.

When she reappeared I said, 'What about your husband? I

saw him, you know.' And I described the man walking on his
toes through her room.

'Ah . . . Yes, him,' Mariella said, looking at me in such a
strange way that momentarily I thought that the telephone call
must have brought bad news, something unexpected. Then she
laughed suddenly, I suppose at my glum face, and said: 'Don't
let's waste time on him! Have you ever been to the fish market
here? If you are interested we could go this afternoon?'

The fish were landed on a beach a tram-ride away, carried up
to the quay and displayed in boxes and squirming heaps on the
concrete floor of the municipal market hall. Serious bidders
sat in the front row of tiered green benches, or stood bunched
together shouting and gesticulating to one another about the
catch. Spectators like us sat high up on either side of a precip-
itous gallery directly under the glass roof.

The auction had been in progress for over an hour when
I became aware that surreptitiously Mariella was glancing at
her watch, not once or twice but every few minutes.

'Would you like to go?' I asked. The clock on the wall
behind the auctioneer showed a quarter to four; it was very
hot and the smell and the din were overpowering. 'I've had
enough if you have?'

'Four o'clock,' she replied at once. 'At four we'll leave.'

This precision seemed unlike Mariella and it occurred to
me that she was keeping away from the house for a given
length of time, deliberately. Then I dismissed the idea as far-
fetched. Nevertheless, when we did return home I went up to
my room at once, ostensibly to have a bath. The guns hidden
in the chest had gone.

The evening passed quietly enough. Vitor was out and while Mariella prepared supper, I sat on the top step outside the front door watching the sun slowly dip down behind the hibiscus on the wall. I decided that I would telephone my brother later in the evening to ask when he was returning. The business of the guns had unnerved me.

At dinner Mariella seemed subdued, her face pale and strained. In answer to my questions she talked about her home in the north, the kindly faithful people she had known as a child, how different her life had become. She mentioned Vitor several times and the fact that he had not returned. Judging by her expression they were still having their quarrel. At eleven, I asked if I might telephone my brother and Mariella dialled the number for me. But she could not get through.

'This country!' she exclaimed. 'Always something!'

The bedroom seemed hot, claustrophobic. I lay awake, thinking about my hostess and her husband. The image of his smiling face as he stood by the bedside was still sharp in my mind. A hunter accustomed to killing, as Sam had put it. Compelling.

The shutters and door onto the balcony were locked, but the windows were open. I got up and locked them; fidgeted restlessly on the wide high bed, the patterns of light cast from the street lamps and car headlights beyond the trees gyrating across the ceiling like huge white birds in flight. When at last I slept I dreamed I was in the plane on the way to La Caicca. From my seat next to the window I could see not cloud and sky, but the dark shadow of trees through which, keeping pace with the plane, bounded a huge wild boar. It was very close: the savage archaic little eyes, folds of flesh covered by sparse black hair, tusks, seemed almost part of the plane itself. I woke full of inexplicable horror to find the room brilliant with morning sunlight even through the shutters.

It was late. Downstairs I found the house deserted. Study, dining room, the formal salon, kitchen all empty. The sink and table in the kitchen were piled with last night's dirty crockery, and when I turned on the taps for water to make coffee, nothing happened: no water. 'This country!' I thought, smiling. Should I go out for coffee to that little place on the square? Then again, perhaps Mariella was in the house somewhere? I could hear a radio on one of the upper floors.

Because of the odd layout of Mariella's house – two parallel buildings jammed together like conjoined twins – point of entry to the inner, older structure at the rear could only be gained from the main staircase at the front. A short passage connected the two halves of the house at second-floor level. Above this, were more floors. The rooms below this extra enclosed space – the other half of the dining room, little study, salon on the ground floor at the front – were closed off; stables accessible only from the courtyard and used to house ancient wooden carts, fodder for animals and the pigeons and rabbits kept in cages by the gardener. The inner rooms above the stables were thus invisible and completely protected by the façade of the house looking out so benignly over courtyard and street.

'We have no need of them at present,' Mariella had said, smiling. 'Not until Vitor marries and I move up there. We leave them empty.'

As I walked up the stairs I heard the radio more distinctly. Music, and someone singing. 'Mariella?' I called from the landing. 'Mariella, are you there?'

Standing in the passage which led from an archway on the stairs, I called her name again, and then Vitor's. But apart from some large insect knocking against a fanlight high up in the wall of the passage, the house was quiet. Unnaturally so, I thought later. When I reached the second archway, set presumably in the wall of the older building, I stopped to listen. I could no longer hear the music; it must have come from one of the neighbouring blocks of flats or the courtyard, perhaps. Heat affects sound after all, creates distortions. I noted that the window on the landing where I now stood looked out not onto the garden or courtyard, but crumbling stone or tile; presumably the rear wall of the structure from which I had just come. I stood for a moment studying the layout. These hidden rooms intrigued me, empty and quiet, shut away like this, and it looked innocuous enough, sun flooding down from the floor above. I was trying to establish in my mind the exact position of the blank window in relation to the main house when I heard a sound which froze me in my tracks. Not very far away, perhaps on the further side of the door facing me, a man sneezed, twice.

I realise that since my accident I have become unduly nervous, but for some reason this homely sound almost made me faint with shock; and it was all I could do to turn and walk down the stairs and out into the street without tripping in headlong panic.

At the café on the square I told myself that I was being neurotic, ridiculous. It could be Vitor, someone working in the house, the gardener, housekeeper. (Why did the guns come to mind immediately?)

I had hardly any money on me, so decided that I would go

back briefly to collect my things, spend the day on the beach, then phone my brother in the evening and make arrangements to join him wherever he was. Forget about this bloody house and its occupants. But when I walked into the kitchen, Mariella was standing at the table surrounded by parcels, baskets of shopping.

'That market, the *crowds*! But look, perfect!' She held up a huge pineapple, her face flushed and shining with pleasure. 'I hope Vitor looked after you? The water has been turned off again.'

'Yes. Mariella,' I began. 'Those rooms upstairs – is someone living up there?'

'They are empty,' she replied almost at once but quite calmly. 'Why?'

'I heard something . . . Someone.'

'Probably the dog. One of our dogs is ill. I had to shut him away up there, away from the others.' The improbability of this combined with her candid smiling gaze made me lower my eyes. 'The vet is coming soon, so I have to remain here. Do you have any plans for today?' She began to sort fruit and vegetables onto the table. 'An exhibition perhaps? The museum is not far.'

It was clear that Mariella wanted me out of the house, but I hadn't the peace of mind necessary for looking at paintings. I told her that I would go and have a quiet investigatory look at the neighbourhood. I bought pancakes from a street vendor, wondering whether it was wise, and idled away the afternoon on the beach. Swam, lay on the sand, swam again, had a coffee and a cognac at one of the ramshackle little fish bars perched like driftwood on the shore; sat watching a procession of fishing boats negotiate the buoys laced together across the bay. I was reluctant to return to the house but couldn't think of an alternative. Perhaps Sam could join us earlier than we had originally planned? I decided to telephone him as soon as I got back.

Vitor and his mother looked startled, as if they had never seen me before, when I interrupted what was obviously another confrontation. I could hear their raised voices as I walked towards the kitchen door. Mariella switched to English immediately when she saw me.

'Ah, you are back! Did you go to the exhibition?' And then sotto voce to Vitor: 'It is easy for you.'

'*You – have – to – choose!*' Each word was emphasised equally and the passion in his voice was unmistakable. Politics again, I thought. Arrogant young prig.

'Between what?' I asked, walking round the table. 'Choices are often more difficult as one gets older, Vitor. The result of wisdom.'

He turned, and for a moment I thought he was going to hit me. Then he picked up his cap and strode out of the room, slamming the door after him. Mariella began to cry.

'Let's go out to dinner, Mariella,' I said. 'I'll treat you.'

'There are things . . . The dog.' She glanced at her watch, at me in a distracted way, started to say something, then changed her mind.

'It will do you good, Mariella. But first I want to telephone Sam.'

'The telephones have not been working since yesterday.' She sounded desperate.

★

Mariella took me to the old quarter, a decaying densely-packed maze of alleys, narrow rocketing streets perched above the harbour. Here the slogans were twenty-foot high, dogs rooted in the gutters among the rubbish and women shouted to one another across lines of washing hanging like sails above our heads.

The restaurant was in a dark cellar of a place run by recently returned 'colons'. The man who came to serve us looked Indian, Gujerati perhaps.

'But he is Catholic and speaks the same language as me,' whispered Mariella.

We were the only white-skinned customers and the only women. By myself I would never have ventured into such a place. But Mariella seemed completely at home, immediately entering into conversation with a man at the next table, a fat brown baby in his arms.

'I was asking if he knew anybody who would come to help us with our grape harvest,' Mariella said, smiling. 'He is a policeman off duty. He says there is some sort of strike planned and they are expecting trouble, otherwise he would ask his cousin who has no work. They are going to use the barracks as polling stations during the election,' she added, stroking the baby's soft plump wrist.

'Will that affect Vitor?' I asked.

'He is in a mobile battery. No, I don't think so.' Mariella gazed at the baby laughing on its father's knee. 'Vitor wants to tear everything down.'

'Everything?'

'Everything that matters.'

'He is young,' I said. 'I expect it is difficult for him, coming back like this. He'll change. Do you think they have a telephone that works here?'

'Use my mobile. You might get through.'

Sam's number rang alright but he had not yet come in, back from his work. I left my name and said I was trying to contact him.

'You see! Vitor is not here,' Mariella said the moment we were in the hall and had called up the stairs once or twice.

'He has been out – like us. He'll be back.'

'I wish it was as simple as that,' Mariella said.

Again I slept badly, waking in a sweat from another nightmare. It is this house, I thought. I must get away from this house.

Mariella was in the kitchen when I went down in the morning, and I could see at a glance that the depressed mood of the previous evening had lifted.

'Vitor back?' I asked, but she hardly seemed to hear me.

'What are you going to do today? You mustn't waste your time. What about that exhibition? It closes tomorrow.' Through the open door we both heard the telephone begin to ring in the hall.

'The vet!' Mariella said over shoulder, but in a moment she stood in the doorway again. 'It's Sam – wants to speak to you, long distance.'

The line was bad. 'Are you alright?' I heard him say. Then, unaccountably, 'There's nothing to worry about.'

'Worry? About what? Sam?'

But he hurried on as if he hadn't heard me. 'It's only a few of them. Your part of the city isn't affected.'

'What? What city?' I repeated stupidly.

'Don't go into the centre,' my brother said. 'Keep with Mariella. I'll be back as soon as I can.'

'What's happened? What are you talking about?' I was beginning to be alarmed.

'Some kind of revolt.' His voice was getting fainter. 'Nobody knows what's going on. Looks like the air force this time. Nothing much. Small —' At this point the line clicked sharply and he was cut off.

'Sam?' I was left holding the buzzing receiver.

'Where is he?' Mariella stood behind me.

'He was talking about some kind of revolt or something. Trouble,' I said.

'Oh there's always trouble in this country. The military commander has been dismissed so they turn the water off!' She burst out laughing, shaking her hair back from her face. How incredibly young she looks, I thought. Beautiful. No wonder Sam is still in love with her.

'When is Sam arriving?' she asked suddenly.

'Soon. He said to stay near you, here. What has actually happened?'

'The naval barracks have been taken over . . . Last night. Probably the government will fall. Perhaps they have the TV and radio stations as well this time.' She switched on the little portable standing on the window sill and listened attentively. 'No, that's all OK still.' She spread her arms and laughed again. 'All talk,' she said. 'Nothing changes. You go to your exhibition — it is only across the square. And I'll wait for the vet, again!' She smiled at me, apparently quite unperturbed, and I was convinced. God knows why.

★

The main square of the district, a few streets away from Mariella's house, seemed exactly as before and full of people. Old men in the shade of the plane trees with their dominoes; children calling to each other, scuffing the dusty gravel as they raced about on bicycles; laden women in their perpetual black walking slowly to or from the market; businessmen, sailors, a few dark-skinned soldiers in striped and spotted camouflage. Then, through a gap in the dense shade and foliage of the trees on the further side of the square, I saw clusters of armed soldiers at a barricade, stopping cars on the road which led out of the city. I changed direction and walked up the steps which led to a broad gravelled terrace or belvedere in front of the massive stone basilica, now the Catholic church.

As I reached the terrace, I heard a distant explosion, then another. The crowd below me in the square faltered, stopped, turned in the direction from which these sounds came. Again there was a sudden detonation, much louder, and I heard the whining of a small aeroplane, very low. Men shouted at each other across the crowd, women screamed, and from the other side of the square came the dry rattle of gunfire. I stepped back from the balustrade quickly and ran into the church.

It was dark and cold in there after the heat of the square, and surprisingly empty – although one or two people followed me in. Two nuns knelt on the stone floor in a patch of sunlight, their heads bowed, and a few black-shawled elderly women turned at my unceremonial entry, crossing themselves. I sat down near the shrine of the Madonna, her candles wavering in the draught from the door, as sirens wailed in the distance. There were more intermittent explosions and I heard some firing, but it felt safer in here.

I have no idea how long I sat there. An hour, two hours, three? By the time I had made up my mind to move I had grown cold and was shivering. Outside, the light was blinding and, because of the crowds gathered on the steps of the church, I couldn't see as far as the square or what was happening there. I decided the best thing would be to go back to the house.

The gates were locked. I had to ring several times before the housekeeper emerged, shuffling down the steps behind the *Datura* trees. She stared at me through the bars, gesticulating and rattling the keys as she pointed back over my head at the city. I knew she was asking me questions but I could neither understand nor answer her. I looked at my watch. It was three o'clock.

Mariella was still out, it seemed. The downstairs rooms were deserted and I wasn't going to try again upstairs. The water had come on, so I made coffee, took some cheese, bread and an apple from the pantry, brought Mariella's little radio to the table and switched it on. Pop music and a babble of unintelligible language and then, as I fiddled with the knobs, an English voice, clear and unhurried – presumably some sort of overseas news. I listened for some time and sure enough eventually it came: 'The situation appears confused –' The announcer sounded bored. 'There has been sporadic shelling by artillery during the day, but the city is now quiet. The leaders of the rebellion are thought to be in control of air-force headquarters. The attitude of other operational units is unknown although the best-equipped units of the armed forces are thought to be those loyal to the government.' It sounded familiar enough. I wondered if I had got the right country.

The city did not seem all that quiet to me. Muffled explosions continued and the sirens screaming in the streets set my teeth on edge. Restlessly I wandered in and out of the kitchen, the hall, stood by the window in Mariella's little study; saw the housekeeper let herself out of the courtyard gate. I thought of running after her, but decided against it. Just before six, things seemed to get a bit calmer. I got up to fetch the radio and heard footsteps. At last, I thought with intense relief and ran to open the study door. Two soldiers, their uniforms, hair, even their weapons powdered over with fine grey dust and grit, crashed swaying into the room supporting another man between them. Mariella's husband.

He could hardly stand, and his eyes kept closing in a face so white and drained I could see the prodigious effort to remain conscious. A huge bloody patch showed on one side of his tunic, extending from his waist over the hip and upper leg. Feebly he took a step towards the couch and his companions helped him onto it. The younger one, little more than a boy, began to harangue me in a rough, almost hysterical voice.

'English,' I said. 'Please, I don't understand.'

'Mariella?' the other man asked at once. He was older, greyhaired. 'Where? She . . . ?'

I shook my head. 'I don't know.'

The younger one went to the window and closed the shutters, lit a cigarette and stood there smoking. One side of his face was grazed and bleeding, smudged with dirt. He looked exhausted.

'Water?' murmured the soldier kneeling by the couch.

Mariella always kept fresh water in the cool of the pantry – 'for emergencies', as she put it, laughing, and I went to fetch some. The soldier bent to help the man on the couch, cradling his head and gazing into his face as he tried to drink. The boy at the window made some remark, stabbed his cigarette towards the courtyard, gesticulating nervously. But his companion did not reply, merely continued to gaze at the man he held in his arms, scrutinising his face.

Some minutes passed. At length the soldier on his knees crossed himself and stood up.

'Going now,' he said quietly.

'Going?' I echoed, almost shouting. 'Where? Where are you going? I am alone here. You can't just leave him like that!' I picked up the phone on Mariella's desk. 'He should be in hospital. Phone the hospital!'

He took the telephone from me, listened for a moment and offered it back. It was dead, of course.

There was a noise, a disturbance in the street outside, dogs barking. At once, the two men turned to the window, hands on their weapons, waiting tensely as if they expected someone at the gate. Nobody came and they relaxed again. That's it, I thought. They are on the run. They have brought him here, somehow, the only safe place they could think of, and now they are going. They have to, they can't wait for Mariella.

After they had gone I stood paralysed. The room smelt of blood. And he's a doctor, I thought. Why is he wearing a uniform?

In the kitchen I poured out a large glass of brandy and swallowed it down, choking; found what I needed: scissors, water, something to tear into bandages. He was muttering incoherently, eyes closed. I forced brandy into him, took off his tie and loosened his collar, then undid the tunic and waistband.

It was appalling, like meat. I gulped down more brandy and started. Swabbed and cut away the blood-sodden clothing, wiped the outer edges of the lacerated mess of gashes and holes. I didn't dare do any more – laid strips of linen across his groin, thigh oozing blood, covered it all with a clean towel. He seemed very cold, so I doubled up one of Mariella's beautiful peasant shawls which hung on the wall and laid it over him; eased off his boots, which stuck out incongruously from the end of the couch.

He was ghastly pale, grey, spikes of damp black hair sticking to his forehead. Momentarily I wondered if he was still breathing, but as I bent over him, watching uneasily, he opened his eyes, fierce, black, brilliant eyes, and stared at me. He was trying to speak. I knelt down close and took his hands, ice-cold, and held them. I could only just make out the whispered words:

'*Mariella?*' It was an immense effort. He closed his eyes again, lay without moving.

'She'll be here soon. Soon,' I said.

Where the bloody hell was that woman? Still holding his hands, I wedged myself between the wall and the end of the couch and settled down to wait; for what or who I had no idea. I must have dropped off, the brandy probably – and when I woke with a start, stiff and disorientated, Vitor crouched beside me, shaking my arm, watched by two soldiers standing in the doorway.

'Have the police been here?'

'Police?' I stared at him, confused. He was unshaven and dirty, somehow older.

'Yes! Anyone?' He waved the revolver he held in one hand.

'No. Vitor.' With an effort – my legs were cramped and awkward – I got to my feet. 'Vitor, your father –' I glanced down at the couch: he was still breathing. 'Where is Mariella?'

'At the American Embassy.'

'You *must* get a doctor!' He did not reply, and I stumbled on, trying to explain. 'I – I am so sorry. I did what I could, but –'

'I hope he dies,' Vitor said, his voice cold, flat. He walked over to the window and stood there looking out and balancing his revolver in one hand.

Exactly at that moment my brother Sam walked into the room.

I was beyond speech and hardly heard the brief exchange between Vitor and my brother, which anyway was not in English. I clung to Sam like a child, sobbing, incoherent.

'The hospital! He must see a doctor –'

'They are coming,' he said, putting an arm round me, and indeed, as he spoke I heard a siren screaming through nearby streets. 'Sounds like an ambulance,' Sam said. 'Let's hope it is ours.'

But we had to wait another half an hour before we heard voices, the clatter of boots, and Mariella's study door opened to admit a nurse, two more soldiers and a tall bulky middle-aged man: the doctor. I felt the ordinary common-sense world ebbing away as I realised he had the same features, the same powerfully muscled body, big head and dark hair, eyes, as the man on the couch. They were so alike they were identical except for the clothes.

I looked from Vitor to my brother and back to the doctor now lifting the shawl and opening his leather case.

'So this is the end of it,' Sam said quietly, more to himself than me, his eyes fixed on Vitor's impassive unshaven face.

'My father' – Vitor gestured toward the newcomer – 'has come to attend to his brother, my uncle. My mother's lover.' His voice seemed loud in the quiet room. 'My family,' he added with extreme bitterness.

With the doctor's car and the ambulance waiting at the gates, they carried him down the steps and across the courtyard on a stretcher. We stood and watched by the window. I don't know whether he was still alive.

'Sam –'

'Twins,' my brother said, 'like us, but identical. An old story.'

I was silent, something niggling at the back of my mind.

'That uniform,' I began.

'Air force.' Sam's face was expressionless. 'A colonel in the air force. Attractive devil. No woman could resist him.'

A stranger, I thought, nothing to me. Aloud I said, 'Sam, someone had weapons hidden here.'

'Yes, I expect so. Everyone has them in this country.'

Neither of us spoke for a while, then Sam said:

'You realise it was Vitor's battery? Shelling the buildings they were in?'

'Did he know? That they were there? Or . . . ' My voice trailed away.

Sam said nothing, staring across the empty courtyard, the garish street beyond the *Datura* trees. Images of that handsome pallid face beaded with sweat persisted obstinately. Nothing, nothing to me, I thought. Forget it.

'Are you in love with Mariella, Sam?' I asked. No reply. Perhaps he did not hear me.

We stood side by side gazing out of the window. Above the courtyard a dull glow of red punctuated by flashes of gunfire and thin trails of tracer illumined the dark sky. Presumably Sam was thinking the same as me. Did Vitor know where his uncle was likely to be during those few short hours? And had he seen to it somehow that those particular buildings had been targeted and reduced to rubble, almost everybody in them killed? And if he knew where his uncle was – as I am sure he did – who told him? Now that Mariella is my sister-in-law I suppose I could ask her, but as yet I have not been able to do so.

'I'll get her out,' Sam said, still staring down at the courtyard below. 'Somehow.' His eyes were fixed, very wide open, and it occurred to me for the first time that he was very much more involved in it all than I had realised. I wondered what he knew exactly.

The telephone on Mariella's desk rang, two short bursts, and then stopped. I picked it up but of course no one answered. Sam took out his mobile and began to dial.

'I'll try the embassy, I have a special number.'

'If we could just leave, Sam?'

But we had to stay on in the house until the following day, when four heavily-armed marines came in a jeep. Forty-eight hours later the three of us, Sam, Mariella and I, were flown out in a United States Army transport plane.

Vitor and his uncle are both dead. The uncle either before or on his way to hospital; Vitor shot by a sniper marksman as, an easy target, he rode in his armoured car through the city centre six months later, part of the victory parade. His father, who I only met the one time, still works in the rheumatology department at the City Hospital. Sam and Mariella have been married for a year now. They seem happy, although Mariella says she misses the sun. We never discuss the recent past.

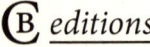 *editions*

Founded in 2007, CB editions publishes chiefly short fiction and poetry, including work in translation.

Books can be ordered from www.cbeditions.com.